CHARMED AND DANGEROUS
THE RISE OF THE PRETTY COMMITTEE

CLIQUE novels by Lisi Harrison:

THE CLIQUE

BEST FRIENDS FOR NEVER

REVENGE OF THE WANNABES

INVASION OF THE BOY SNATCHERS

THE PRETTY COMMITTEE STRIKES BACK

DIAL L FOR LOSER

IT'S NOT EASY BEING MEAN

SEALED WITH A DISS

BRATFEST AT TIFFANY'S

THE CLIQUE SUMMER COLLECTION

P.S. I LOATHE YOU

BOYS R US

CHARMED AND DANGEROUS

Also by Lisi Harrison:

ALPHAS

THE CLIQUE PREQUEL
BY LISI HARRISON

poppy

LITTLE, BROWN AND COMPANY
New York   Boston

Poppy

Little, Brown and Company
Hachette Book Group
237 Park Avenue, New York, NY 10017
For more of your favorite series, go to www.pickapoppy.com

First Edition: October 2009
First International Edition: October 2009

Poppy is an imprint of Little, Brown and Company.
The Poppy name and logo are trademarks of Hachette Book Group, Inc.

Cover design by Andrea C. Uva
Cover photos by Roger Moenks
Author photo by Gillian Crane

alloy**entertainment**

Produced by Alloy Entertainment
151 West 26th Street, New York, NY 10001

ISBN: 978-0-316-05537-6

10 9 8 7 6 5 4 3 2 1
RRD-C
Printed in the United States of America

For the Clique fans who supported me along the way,
even when I had type-os. I ah-dore you all.

"Bonne annéeeeeee!" Kendra Block trilled into the phone with gushing enthusiasm.

"Happy New Year, darling!" Massie's father added over swirling laughter, clinking champagne flutes, and strains of "Auld Lang Syne." "We love you!"

"I love you tooooo!" Massie shouted back. But from the stillness of her crisp navy blue and white bedroom those words sounded hollow, lonely, forced; like whoo-hooing on a private riding trail after a blanketing snowfall.

She eyed the swamp green screen on her Motorola flip phone.

Was it really midnight in Paris?

It was like her mom and dad had ridden a time machine six hours into the future. Even though they were parents, Massie envied them. They already knew whether their night was magical: whether their outfits would inspire copycats . . . whether their jokes were LOL-worthy . . . whether their conversation topics were charming . . . whether their New Year's Eve story had a happy ending . . . whether—

"Where are you?" Kendra asked, oozing giddiness.

"M'room." Massie plopped onto the edge of her navy duvet and flexed her toes. *Was silver polish fun or done? Class or crass? Mature or manure? Gawd, if only there was some kind of list that told girls what was in and what was out. . . .*

"Open your door." Kendra giggled.

"Huh? Why?"

"Go!" Kendra insisted with mock frustration.

Massie slid off the edge of her bed, her gold silk kimono sparking and snapping with static electricity.

"Does she like it?" William asked in the background.

"Shhhhh," Kendra hissed. "She hasn't seen it yet."

Massie squeaked with burst-at-the-seams impatience.

"Is the door open? Are you there yet?" Kendra asked.

"Almost." Massie padded across the white wool rug, heart revving. *Was it the tiny black pug she had been begging for? Oh, puh-leaase make it the tiny black pug she had been begging for! With a big red bow atop her mini head and a diamond anklet with a bone charm.* That would semi-make up for her mother's holiday "surprise" where she'd transformed Massie's three-shades-of-pink boudoir into a showroom for Tommy Hilfiger. Blue, red, and white everything. It put the *nawt* in nautical. But she decided to put up with it because the decorator assured her it was "fresh" and Massie's best friends agreed.

"Okay, I'm here." She gripped the brass anchor–shaped doorknob.

"Yayyyyyyyyy!" screeched Kendra. "Openit! Openit! Openit!"

Turning the anchor slowly, so as not to startle the pup, Massie cracked the door and peered out. Expecting a nose full of new-puppy smell, she inhaled deeply. All she got was the sharp floral scent of Crabtree & Evelyn's Spring Rain home spray, her mom's favorite.

Massie lowered her gaze, ready to make contact with a pair of moist black eyes. Eyes that would pulsate hearts for her new master and—

"Ew!" she blurted at the sudden appearance of a woman's bare feet. Size nine. Calloused. Dry. Neglected.

A plaid flannel nightgown skimmed the woman's ankles and tented her stocky body. Strands of long black hair, freed from their tight bun but contorted from hours of captivity, clung to the glistening Pond's cold cream slathered on the side of her face.

"Inez?"

"Happy New Year." She held a Tiffany box in her palm and smiled warmly.

Ignoring the housekeeper, Massie peered left, then right. Was the pug hiding? Was she part two of her parents' guilt gift? Was the blue box a red herring?

But, as usual, nothing in the hallway seemed out of

place. The only panting came from Inez, who must have been instructed to run up the winding staircase before Massie opened the door.

"Do you love it?" her mother asked.

"Does she love it?" her father echoed.

Sensing Massie's paralyzing disappointment, Inez opened the box for her. "Beauuuutiful." The housekeeper dangled the glistening gold charm bracelet under Massie's jutting chin.

"It has all of your favorite things on it," Kendra explained. "A high-heeled shoe, a dollar sign, a horse, a diamond-encrusted bell—for the diamonds, obviously, not the bell—and a pig."

"A *pig*?"

"Yes, you wanted one for Christmas, only we've had the hardest time finding housebroken breeds so we—"

"Mohhhm, I wanted a *pug*, nawt a *pig*."

Kendra gasped in horror. "William," she called into the party noise. "She wanted a *pug*, not a *pig*! . . . I know . . . *huge* relief!" Her lips returned to the mouthpiece. "Those are so much easier to find, darling. We'll get one as soon as we return to the *États-Unis*."

"Yay!" Massie pinched the bracelet off Inez's finger and slid it on. It was a little loose, but nothing she couldn't have Mr. Novick, the family jeweler, fix after the holidays. She examined her wrist from all angles, study-

4

ing the way the light reflected off the chain. Aside from the mistaken-bacon it was actually kinda cute. And no one else had one . . . yet.

Fireworks soared and popped on the other end of the call. Massie felt like exploding right along with them. She was finally going to get a puppy! A confidant. A real best friend. A sibling.

"Oh, and we got you a tiny gold Eiffel Tower. It's ab-so-lutely chaaarming." Kendra giggled at her corny pun.

Massie's phone beeped.

The swamp green screen flashed AHNNA.

Her palms began to sweat.

One last firecracker whistled in the background, then fizzled out.

The phone beeped again.

Ignoring the call would mean violating Ahnna's strict "talk or walk" policy, an offense that would put Massie in social solitary for an entire weekend. No phone calls, e-mails, IMs, or gossip alerts. She had to act.

Now.

"SoundsgreatMomIcan'twaitHappyNewYearIloveyou seeyoutomorrownightbyeee."

Click.

"Hullo?" Massie answered quickly. She wave-thanked Inez, then shut the bedroom door.

"Vicky and Sheldon'll be pulling up in five," barked the girl on the other end.

The line went dead.

With quaking thumbs, Massie set the stopwatch on her Motorola, then tossed it on her bed. Thankfully, her dark, glossy hair had been professionally twisted into a loose chignon hours ago. Cheeks were tinted to a flirty blush. Lips shimmered with rose-scented gloss. And the faceless mannequin in the corner of her bedroom looked festive times ten in an Agnès B. dress, with a shiny black ticket lodged between her thin porcelain fingers.

Massie slid the gold charm bracelet onto her model's stiff white arm and stepped back to evaluate. Head cocked, she finger-tapped her chin.

"Hmmmmmmmm." She sighed. "Something is awf. Not awful, just awf."

The black minidress stamped with silver metallic triangles hung like couture. Gunmetal gray Prada wedges and black cashmere kneesocks would add just the right amount of funk to the function. And the coveted ticket to famed talk-show host Merri-Lee Marvil's celebrity-studded *New Year's Yves* broadcast—where a one-of-a-kind Yves Saint Laurent beaded clutch would drop at midnight like the Times Square ball—was the perfect accessory.

Soooooo . . . chin-tap . . . chin-tap . . . chin-tap . . .

What was it? What was putting the "out" in her outfit?

The soft yellow light from her bedside lantern reflected off the charm bracelet and winked at her. The new kid was trying to tell her something.

Ehmagawd, GOLD!

The gold charm bracelet clashed with the silver triangles on the dress and gunmetal gray shoes. It was like chewing mint gum and drinking Diet Coke. It was a bitter combination. And the last thing she needed was for people in India or Cairo (or wherever) to be watching Merri-Lee Marvil's celebrity-studded *New Year's Yves* broadcast and saying that some American was mixing metals. And if *they* noticed, Ahnna would *definitely* notice.

Massie glanced at her phone—00:02:16:23.

Ehmagawd! Only two minutes, sixteen seconds, and twenty-three whatevers left!

She could ditch the bracelet, but it was new. And gold. And totally enviable. It could start trends or, at the very least, conversations. But rethink the Agnès B.? At *this* hour? Impossible.

Anxiety ravaged her flesh like razor burn.

Whattodo? Whattodo? Whattodo?

And then, in a stroke of brilliance, Massie pinned her gold *M* brooch to one sock, and a gold *B* to the other.

The initial pins were a perfect way to tie the whole thing together. After a quick digital picture of the outfit—to avoid duplication in the future—Massie tore the clothes off her body double and speed-dressed. Just as she was sliding the bracelet up her thin wrist, BMW tires crunched the gravel on her driveway.

Her alarm beeped—00:00:00:00.

Inez's voice came over the white intercom on her nightstand. "The Pinchers are here."

Massie smoothed her dress. "Nine-seven," she rated herself out of ten, docking point three for her pale December skin. Satisfied, she turned away from her otherwise flawless reflection.

Racing down the stairs Massie blinked back the cyclone of questions twisting through her brain. Would Ahnna approve of her clothes or turn up her nose? Would she make memories or enemies? Would mixed metals set trends or disgust friends?

Ahhhh, to be in France and already have all the answers.

"Stop!" Ahnna shouted.

"*What?*" Mr. Pincher slammed on the brakes.

Ahnna, Lana, Shauna, Brianna, and Massie lurched forward. They slammed into the tan leather seats and then busted out laughing.

"What *happened*?" Mr. Pincher turned to face Ahnna, his white cashmere scarf swaddling his cleft chin. "Is everyone okay?"

A stunned Mrs. Pincher gripped her pearl choker and glared out the windshield.

"*Okay?* Uv'korse we're oh-*kay*." Ahnna lowered her window. Bitter cold wind blew her butterscotch blond curls around like the fur of a goldendoodle on an air-sniffing joy ride. "This is gonna be the coolest party evv."

Massie nodded in agreement while massaging her cramped calf. Squeezing into the back of a Beemer with three other girls hardly said *New Year's Eve*; more like *hitchhiking to the nearest town for gas*. She'd offered Isaac, her driver, and their new Lexus LX 470 with the stocked fridge, killer speakers, and heated seats (to keep dresses from wrinkling). But Ahnna had flat-out refused.

No shock there. When Massie suggested it, Ahnna turned it down.

They drove under a New Year's Yves sign made of silver and gold Swarovski crystals and entered the packed parking lot. Normally reserved for private planes and helicopters, the tarmac had been transformed into what looked like a luxury car showroom.

Rows of just-washed luxury sedans glistened with pride, awaiting their drivers' return. Or were they glistening with *sweat*? Sweat from knowing that with a new year comes a new model, and they were days away from being traded in?

Massie's insides sank under the weight of her sympathy. She knew that you-could-be-replaced-in-a-heartbeat feeling all too well.

"Stawp!" Brianna smacked Shauna's arm. "Check out the license plate on that Bentley."

Shauna repositioned her cherry red Moschino glasses. "It says J-Lo!"

"Stawp!" Lana squealed.

"M'gawsh!" Ahnna clenched her fists.

"When did 'stop' stop meaning *stop*?" Mr. Pincher tapped the gas and inched toward the valet attendant.

"I hear it's even better on the inside," Mrs. Pincher told them as they pulled past the snaking line of ticketless wannabes hoping to convince the bouncers to let them in.

"Eeeeeeeeeeee!" Ahnna, Shauna, Lana, and Brianna shook their hands as if drying manicures. They did it every time they were excited times ten. Massie, however, refused. It didn't look hot—it looked like they were on fire.

"You guys should really calm down," Massie whispered from the side of her glossy mouth. "You're acting like you've never been to a TV event before."

Ahnna pulled her head inside the car, her windblown curls now a wild mane. "And you *have*?"

"No," Massie mouthed, eyeing the sprawling airplane hangar, which by now probably contained half of America's A-list, and most of Britain's. "But *they* don't know that." She waved her hand toward the wannabes and— "Oops!"—her bracelet accidentally slid off her wrist, landing on the car carpet with a jingle-thud.

"What was *that*?" Shauna thumb-pressed her red glasses against her nose and scanned the floor.

"My new *Tiffany* charm bracelet." Massie scooped it up and slid it back on.

Lana, Shauna, and Brianna looked at Ahnna, their eyes filled with the longing of a child silent-begging Mom for a slice of chocolate cake.

Yes! They liked it!

"Whatevs." Ahnna rolled her eyes. "I used to have one of those in the second grade."

"You *did*?" Mrs. Pincher turned around to face her daughter, her thin eyebrows arched in genuine surprise. "I don't remember that."

Ahnna's cheeks reddened.

Respectfully, Lana, Shauna, and Brianna pretended not to notice. Massie turned toward the window with smug satisfaction.

Sticking it to Ahnna felt better than proving a teacher wrong or buying an outfit before it showed up in *Us Weekly*. Yet, in the spaces behind her rapidly beating heart, where everything was quiet and true, Massie knew it wasn't right.

She should want the best for her best friend; *have* her back, not stab it. But Ahnna made that so hard, especially when she vetoed all of Massie's good ideas—even the ones that would up their social standing at Presbyterian Elementary and Middle School (or PMS, as everyone called it because its students were so moody) to alpha- and beta-fy PMS's super-popular LMNOP (Lysa, Madison, Nylah, Opal, and Peyton).

Lately it had been so bad, Massie had started keeping a list. It detailed all of the suggestions she made and the reasons Ahnna knocked them down, just in case she ever wanted to sue for "obstruction of popularity," aka "pop-blocking."

DATE	MASSIE'S SUGGESTION	AHNNA'S RESPONSE	WHAT SHE REALLY MEANS
12.1	I am going to Paris with my parents for New Year's. They said I could bring you guys. Wanna go?	I can't. I already have tickets for Merri-Lee Marvil's *New Year's Yves* party. My dad can get tickets for all of you. He's the director of her daily talk show so it shouldn't be a problem.	I will do whatever it takes to make sure you don't go with Shauna, Brianna, and Lana while I'm stuck here. Even if it means inviting you to a party I was going to use to make you jealous. Besides, I want to shop-block you and keep you from the incredible stores on Avenue Champs-Élysées. If I have to buy my Chanel at Saks, so should everyone. Oh, and have I mentioned in the last eight seconds that my dad is the director of *The Daily Grind*? I have? Oops. My bad.
12.3	Let's meet before every holiday party to plan our wardrobes. PMS is a uniform school. We are behind other schools when it comes to fashion. We can combine our clothes, put together outfits, and style each other so we all look ah-mazing.	I don't decide what I'm going to wear until day of. Sometimes minute of. Sorry.	I'm getting help from Yasmine, Merri-Lee's stylist, and I don't want her to help you. Every Ahnnabee for herself. *Uh-kay?*
12.11	Let's have sleepovers at my house every Friday night.	My parents will never approve. They like me at home.	I hate being reminded that your house is bigger/nicer/smells cleaner/is better staffed than mine.
12.11	So let's have sleepovers at *your* house every Friday night.	My parents are private and don't like guests.	I still suck my thumb.

DATE	MASSIE'S SUGGESTION	AHNNA'S RESPONSE	WHAT SHE REALLY MEANS
12.19	I don't think we should wear so much eyeliner. It's all about cheeks and lips.	Tell that to Shauna who just got glasses and needs a little something to make her feel less pathetic.	I put on my older sister's eyeliner at the beginning of the school year and everyone thought I was in the sixth grade. Does anyone think you're in the sixth grade? No? Didn't think so.
12.20	Let's change our name. The Ahnnabees sounds kinda desperate, like we're wannabes or something.	You're just saying that because you don't have an *ahna* name like me, Lana, Shauna, and Brianna and you're jealous.	I managed to convince four girls to name a clique after *me*. Do you hawnestly think I'm going to change it?
12.24	Let's play a game called "What Would You Rather Get for Christmas?"	Okay, I'll start. What would you rather get for Christmas? This stupid game or something fun?	No.

"We're here," Mr. Pincher announced, opening the door and dropping his keys in the white-gloved hands of the parking attendant.

Massie shimmied out of her maxi shearling and followed the others outside. Without shame, the Ahnnabees hurried toward the entrance, each in a different-color puffy jacket: yellow, pink, baby blue, and lilac. They looked like a gang of skinny-legged Easter-colored M&M's from the commercials.

Over the years, Massie had told them winter coats were party-dress poison. But tonight she decided to let it go. She was over them treating her words of wisdom like sunflower seeds, something to chew on for a second and then spit out. Instead, she raced for the warmth of the giant klieg lights by the entrance, proud to know she stood apart.

A crowd of bundled-up regular people was gazing in awe at the clear night sky. Or rather, at the crystal-covered pole that jutted out from the center of the airplane hangar and the massive gold-and-black beaded YSL clutch affixed to the top. Their chapped lips were agape and puffs of mouth smoke filled the frigid night air, as if they were beholding the star atop the Christmas tree at Rockefeller Center, or an alien landing.

Like a true celebrity, Massie avoided their eyes as she breezed by, casually waving her black ticket as if it were nothing more than a tissue.

"Stawp!" Ahnna blurted when they came upon two sumo wrestlers-slash-doormen in white tuxedos and white (faux?) fur hats. Their massive suits doubled as screens that broadcast the party, live—and were currently featuring a performance by Mandy Moore. It was a little something Merri-Lee insisted on doing for her poor freezing fans who hadn't been lucky enough to win access during her monthlong on-air giveaway.

The Pincher party flashed their tickets and the sumo wrestlers opened the doors.

"Eeeeeeeee," screeched the Ahnnabees as they entered the enormous space. Usually the stark home to a fleet of American Airlines jets, the hangar was pulsating with life.

Cameras coasted along tracks, gathering sweeping shots of the beautiful guests as they danced, toasted, and embraced. Servers weaved through the crowd, offering samples of the fantastic dishes prepared over the past year on *The Daily Grind*. Each waitress had the name of her dish, the chef who invented it, and the actual recipe scrawled on her black catsuit in metallic gold pen—handwritten, of course by Freda Luu, winner of Merri-Lee's high school penmanship contest—episode 267—back in May.

The stage, at the far end of the structure, seemed miles away. But the sound of Sisqó asking the audience if they were ready for "The Thong Song" was clear as a well-cut diamond. Massie's insides soared like the Times Square ball in reverse. This was the BPE—Best Party Ever.

"Stawp!" Lana slapped a hand against her mouth, covering the black dot of a mole that punctuated the top left side of her lip. "I love this song!"

"Eeeeeeeee!" The girls squeal-waved. Even Massie did it this time, her charm bracelet sliding off her wrist for the second time.

"Let's go!" The Ahnnabees unzipped their puffy jackets and whipped them toward the rack of hangers, practically blinding the coat-check guy.

"Stawp!" Massie blurted when she saw her four friends dressed in matching Burberry plaid dresses.

"Stawp!" giggled Lana in shock.

"Stawp yourself," gasped Shauna.

"Stawp *your*self," cried Brianna.

"Staw-aw-aaawp!" barked Ahnna. "I can't believe you all copied me!"

A chorus of "we didn't" and "it was a total accident" followed. Massie opened her mouth to reiterate the benefits of pre-party wardrobe summits but what was the point? Ahnna's constipated expression said it all.

"You look like you're wearing the PMS uniform," she finally said, unable to help herself.

"Awwww, aren't they precious?" Mrs. Pincher remarked. "Like a girl group. Who knows, maybe you'll get discovered tonight!"

"Yeah!" Ahnna shouted with glee. "The Ahnnabees!"

"Eeeeeeeeee!" they shrieked again, this time without Massie.

Renewed and ready to take their rightful place by the foot of the stage, they began shoving their way into the crowd.

"*Stop!*" This time the command came from Mr. Pincher.

He casually deposited his empty glass of champagne on a passing server's tray. "We'll be calling you every half hour to make sure you're all safe and accounted for. If you don't answer, I will hunt you down and take you home, midnight or not. Is that clear?"

Ahnna nodded yes and waved her phone to prove she meant it. Then the four girls pranced into the heavily perfumed crowd, bobbing their heads to Sisqó's buoyant hip-hop anthem.

And as usual, Massie trailed behind, like a tag-along sibling or a piece of toilet paper stuck to the bottom of a Jimmy Choo. But wait—comparing the Ahnnabees to fabulous footwear was ten kinds of wrong. They had terrible style, made her feel small, and were cheap. They were the opposite of Jimmy Choos. They were Jimmy Poos. So why was she sticking to their bottoms at all?

The truth was, LMNOP already had an *M*, and the Ahnnabees were the next best thing. During many sleepless nights Massie told herself to stay patient and keep trying. Eventually they'd realize she had good ideas. Great ones, even. And then they'd start treating her better. She wouldn't feel like toilet paper anymore. And the emotional blender in the pit of her stomach would stop churning up feelings of sadness and despair. Maybe they'd even change their name to include hers? Or sleep over? Or compliment her inventive outfits? But that day felt more distant than Uranus.

Pushing past the densely packed partyers, trying to catch up to her so-called friends, Massie was reminded of the turquoise beaded dress she'd bought last year at Saks.

Her mother had been taking her to the Marc Jacobs show during Fashion Week, and Massie was dying to wear something new. The event was about to start, and after an unsuccessful Fifth Avenue blitz and a ton of "hurry up" pressure from Kendra, she agreed to the tacky mini, which was much more figure skater than fashion model. The instant she pushed through the store's revolving door she wanted to return it. But it was too late. The bill had been stamped FINAL SALE in thick red letters. There was no going back. She had settled out of desperation and was stuck with it for life.

Just like the Ahnnabees.

Alicia Rivera bent slowly from the waist, luxuriating in the stretch that warmed her hamstrings and showcased her hyper-flexibility.

"Ahhhhh," she exhaled, rolling a black cashmere leg warmer up her slightly hairy calf.

According to her mother, shaving got a PG-13 rating and was therefore not an option for four more years. One would argue—which Alicia did and did and did— that dancing on one of the biggest television broadcasts of the year would warrant an exception or, at the very least, some Nair. But Nadia Rivera had a very prominent lawyer backing her up: Alicia's father, Len. And they were in the audience, not only to watch their daughter perform, but to make sure her legs were still dusted in unsightly dark hair, just like they were when they left the house.

"What's with the Hot Sox?" Andrea Saunders paced restlessly across the gray carpet in the tiny dressing room. "Were they part of the costume? Because no one told *me* they were part of the costume. And I don't have any." Her cheeks were flushed and her thin, wiry arms were covered in red hives. "Do *you* have any?" She pulled the earbuds out of Brooke Gleason's ears.

"Huh?" Brooke's thin upper lip curled in annoyance.

"Did you bring leg warmers?"

Brooke shook her head no with such conviction her black side-braid smacked her chin. Then she replaced her earbuds, closed her narrow eyes, and lay back on the tattered red love seat she had been dominating for the last thirty minutes.

"Then what are you *doing*?" Andrea grunted. She crossed the dressing room and gripped her stomach, doubling over in pain. "Owwwww! Crrrr-amp."

"I'm the dance captain," Alicia told her reflection. "I should stand out." *And hide my gorilla legs.*

"What? You don't think these costumes stand *out*?" Andrea tugged at her silver sequin–covered tuxedo vest, then smacked her pin-striped short shorts like they were somehow responsible for all of this. "Because *I* sure do!" She grabbed a handful of Lycra from her butt crack. "And besides. You're. Not. The. *Captain!* Skye Hamilton is."

"Well, she's not here now, is she?" Alicia stomped her silver Capezio. "And Mrs. Fossier said while she's gone, I'm *captain*. And I decided that I should wear these, and you shouldn't!" she yelled at Andrea's smooth legs.

It might have been easier if Alicia confessed the whole

hairy reason she needed to cover up. But why should she have to? Until Skye returned from her family vacation to Hawaii, she *was* dance captain. And dance captains shouldn't have to explain.

Not to mention she was legitimately the best dancer in BADSS—Body Alive Dance Studio Squad. But Skye's parents owned the studio *and* she was a year older, so naturally she got the title. But after tonight, everyone would know who really deserved it. And next year everything would be different. Everything would be right.

Suddenly, the room smelled like Egg McMuffin.

Someone triple-knocked on the door and then entered.

"Oh, students, you should *see* how many cameras there are out there!" gushed a petite, prematurely grayhaired woman in desperate need of a haircut and deodorant. But every dancer worth her salt overlooked those details because Mrs. Fossier had performed with Alvin Ailey for four years, and was featured in two coffee-table books. "Do you know how exciting this is? To represent the local culture in Westchester? To . . ." She paused to sniff the air in the tight, windowless dressing room. "What is that smell?"

Alicia and Brooke exchanged a knowing glance. They bit their lips, barely managing to resist hysteria. *Had she finally caught a whiff of her own Danskin?*

"Sorry." Andrea fanned her short shorts. "I'm just a little nervous. I'll be right back."

"Very good." Mrs. Fossier tapped Andrea on the head as she squeezed by.

When she finally returned, Andrea's cheeks were clammy and pale. Hives ravaged the back of her legs.

"How about one more run-through before you go out there and show the world how three young bodies can move as one?" She perched, erect and proud, on the arm of the couch, then began clapping to the metronomic beat in her head. "I'll count you in. Ready?"

Alicia lifted her chin like a confident leader and blinked once for yes. It was time to shut off her brain and let her body do the work. Work that she had been born to do. Work that, after tonight, she would be *paid* to do.

"Wait." Andrea fanned her glistening face. "Does this mean we're going on soon?"

Mrs. Fossier grin-nodded, like someone who couldn't stand to keep a secret for one more minute. "The stage manager should be here shortly to escort us to the stage."

"Ohhhhhhhhhh." Andrea gripped her stomach, which seemed unusually bloated. "I have to go again. I'm not sure I can do this!"

A doughy man with a low ponytail, wearing a black Limp Bizkit concert tee, appeared in the open doorway.

"What do you mean you can't *do* this?" he barked, adjusting the headset to his walkie-talkie. "Aren't you one of the dancers?"

Andrea nodded yes, and then accidentally gave him a taste of her Egg McMuffin. "But I'm kinda getting stage fright."

"I can smell, I mean *tell*." He fanned the air.

Alicia and Brooke burst out laughing.

"Enough!" Mrs. Fossier snapped. "A dancer's body is beautiful no matter how toxic." She looked warmly at Andrea, whose brown eyes were now filling with tears. "You go ahead. The show won't go on without you."

"Maybe it should," Andrea squeaked. "I don't feel so well," she moaned and then sprinted down the hall toward the bathroom.

"It can't," insisted the stage manager. "The director camera-blocked the performance during rehearsal. It's too late to change it now. Either you have three dancers or the Canine Chorus will get to bark two verses of 'Auld Lang Syne' instead of one."

The stage manager consulted his clipboard and made some notes. "You have fifty-two minutes to figure out a solution."

"Done," Alicia blurted, refusing to let the biggest opportunity of her life go to the dogs.

"Where are my girls?" Merri-Lee Marvil stormed into her dressing room and kicked off her five-inch YSL heels. "I need my *girls*." She slid into a pair of pink Ugg clogs and shuffled over to her daughters, snapping her fingers urgently, like their flight was about to board and they were stuck on line at the Starbucks kiosk.

"Over here!" Dylan leapt out from behind the white satin changing screen, thrashing around in spastic homage to the heavy metal song blasting from the stylist's boom box. In her low-rider leather pants, gold YSL wedges, black cashmere tank, and leopard faux-fur collar, she felt sexier than Shakira. Oh yeah! She was ready for her close-up.

"I'm not coming out!" whined her fourteen-year-old sister, Ryan.

"Me either," added Jaime, the thirteen-year-old.

"Why not?" Merri-Lee shouted at the screen, finger-fluffing her red curls.

"They think they look fat." Dylan rolled her green eyes. She was so over her sisters' pathetic weight obsession. Partly because they looked malnourished to begin with, but mostly because it was boring. They never wanted to have giant cookie-baking contests or eat fast food or pound soda and squish the empties. They were too afraid of getting "carby." Not that they would. Dylan did those things all the time and she was still ramen-noodle thin.

"The whole eating-makes-you-fat thing is a lie," she explained for the billionth time. "Advertisers just say that to sell gym memberships and Lean Cuisine."

"If they think *they're* fat, I must be a Pig Newton." Merri-Lee checked the giant digital clock on the wall. The red LCD numbers indicated that she had four minutes and twenty-two seconds left in this commercial break. "I'm coming in," she announced. "Make room for the belly of the ball."

Seconds later, the usual, "You're so thin, no *you're* so thin, no *you* are, I wish, no *I* wish . . ." wafted from behind the changing screen like the fresh-baked smell of sugar-free, low-fat brownies. Dylan ignored her size-two mother and her size-zero sisters and hopped up into the makeup chair so Kali could tame her long red curls. She was about to make her first TV appearance ever. Frizz was not an option.

Facing the mirror, she crossed her legs and—*pop*. The button on her leather pants snapped open. A stomach tsunami surged toward her lap. *Gucci pants should not malfunction like this*, she thought before quickly buttoning them back up.

"Stop moving." Kali lifted the flatiron away from Dylan's head.

"Sorry." Dylan exhaled.

Pop!

The tsunami surged again.

"Yazzz-min!" she managed without moving.

Merri-Lee's longtime stylist stuck her head over the white screen, clutching four safety pins between her lips. "Hmmmm."

"I think you gave me the wrong pants."

"Hmmmm?" Yasmine hummed.

"These are kinda tight." Dylan lifted her pelvis and sucked in her stomach, trying to create space between the digging button and her flesh.

Yasmine spit the pins into her hand and sighed, "The pants are the right size. They look great. You *all* look great. Now stop stressing and finish dressing or you're going to miss your segment."

"She's right," Kali muttered, pressing a chunk of Dylan's hair between the hot clay plates. A puff of steam billowed around her head.

"I'm keeping my whale butt right here where it's safe!" Ryan called. "I don't want to get harpooned."

"Ugggggh," Yasmine groaned, marching toward the full-length mirror, the heels of her black boots click-clacking years of frustration in ways her mouth wouldn't dare. She rolled the mirror toward the girls and huffed, "Look!"

The three Marvils inched out from behind their silky cover.

"*See?*" Yasmine positioned the mirror in front of them. "You're twigs." She rubbed the messy blond hair-bun on top of her head, rolled up her white sleeves, then stuffed her quaking hands in the deep pockets of her black trousers. Yasmine always rocked the hot-woman-in-men's-clothing look. On her, it was sexy. Whenever Dylan tried it she felt like a bar-mitzvah boy.

Merri-Lee cocked her head and examined her reflection. "Hmmm, must be hormones." She cocked to the other side. "I look loads thinner than I feel."

"Me too." Ryan sighed her relief, a strawberry blond tendril twirling in the updraft.

"Same." Jaime shrugged, dismissing her freak-out with the wave of a hand.

"Good." Yasmine wheeled the mirror away, never bothering to put it in front of Dylan, an oversight Dylan took as a compliment. Button-pop or not, the stylist knew the youngest Marvil wasn't a weight watcher. And even though Dylan was slightly curious about the tight Guccis, she refused to let on. Because that would make her like *them*—boring as low-sodium rice crackers.

"Merri-Lee, you're back in a minute thirty," crackled a male voice over the dressing room walkie.

"Blush!" Merri-Lee snapped her fingers.

Kali tossed the flatiron on the makeup-filled table and raced to her boss's side.

"Girls, gather 'round." Merri-Lee sucked in her cheeks for Kali while reaching for her daughters. "Hold." Merri-Lee offered her hands. Jaime grabbed one and Ryan took the other. Dylan forced herself between her sisters like a ring-around-the-rosy reject.

"I want you three to know how proud I am. Not because I host the highest-rated morning talk show in the nation. Or because I landed on my feet after divorcing a man whose fragile ego couldn't cope with a wife that *People* magazine named the thirty-sixth most beautiful woman in Hollywood. But because you are my daughters."

"Awwww," the girls cooed.

"And I can't wait to show the world how gorgeous you are and to thank you in public for bringing *Merri* to my name. Without you, I would simply be Lee. I love you."

"We love *youuuuuuu*," they purred, coming together for a four-way hug.

"Thirty seconds," crackled the voice.

"Gotta jump." Merri-Lee ripped herself away and scampered for her YSL heels. She slid them on and hurried back to the cameras. "See you out there!"

"Kali, can you give me an updo?" Ryan wobbled over to the makeup chair in her gold wedges.

"No, me first." Jaime clomped behind her, her green thong underwear peeking out the back of her leather pants. "I want my hair super-straight and that takes longer."

"What about me?" Dylan screeched, tugging on her half-straight, half-curly hair. "I'm not even done yet."

"You look fine." Ryan jumped into the chair.

"No, she doesn't," said a girl's voice.

Everyone turned.

A dark-haired beauty in a black and silver dress, black kneesocks, and gray Prada wedges stood in the doorway. Hands resting on her narrow hips, she shook her head disapprovingly.

"*What?*" Dylan snapped, not sure if she should hate the intruder for her nerve, or love her for that perfect chignon. "Who are you?"

"Massie Blo—"

"This is a private dressing room!" Yasmine marched toward the door. "You're not allowed back here."

"Sorry. I kinda got lost looking for my friends and then I saw—"

Yasmine was about to slam the door in the girl's face when Dylan stopped her. "Whaddaya mean I don't look *fine*?"

"Those pants are a little . . ." She pursed her shiny lips and tapped her chin. Her amber eyes darted, then rested on Dylan's face. Dylan returned the gaze. They connected for a split second, like two parts of a seat belt that clicked together.

"You know when you squeeze a tube of lip gloss too hard? And some oozes over the top? That's kind of what those pants look like on you. The oozing part."

Ryan and Jaime gasped.

"That's enough!" Yasmine insisted.

"Wait." Dylan held up her palm. "Can I see the mirror?"

Yasmine sighed, then wheeled it over.

After a deep breath of courage, Dylan peeked. She was as long and lean as ever, her leather-clad legs looking like two delicious sticks of black licorice.

"The only thing *oozing* is your jealousy," Dylan told the opinionated stranger.

Her sisters giggled.

"And *your* denial," Massie Blo— fired back.

"And *your* . . ." Dylan walked straight up to the girl and examined her from top to bottom, searching for the ultimate insult. But couldn't find a single thing wrong with her. So she slammed the door in her annoyingly perfect face, then buttoned her leather pants when no one was looking.

She was so tired of girls envy-hating her because she was almost famous. So tired, in fact, that she ate two chocolate brownies, hoping the caffeine in the cocoa might perk her up before showtime.

Pop!

After an hour and thirty-two minutes of breathing through her mouth, Kristen Gregory lost it.

"Does it always smell like beef stew in here?" Her pert nose crinkled in disgust.

"Prob'ly," Ali, her fifteen-year-old cousin, muttered. "I think Mr. Coleman hunts. But I've been babysitting here for so long I'm used to it." She settled into the beige corduroy couch balancing a DVD, a giant glass of Coke, and a bag of mini marshmallows. Without offering Kristen a single thing, she emptied the bag into the soda, pausing while they fizzed in protest.

Kristen stretched out her legs on the glass coffee table and anger-flipped through her math textbook. The only thing worse than being a babysitter's assistant on New Year's Eve was being *treated* like one.

"Shhhhhhhhhh," Ali hissed. "Could you be turning those pages any louder?"

"Huh?" Kristen looked up, shocked.

"I just got Max to sleep." She clicked the video

monitor as proof. A black-and-white image of a crib with a lump inside filled the tiny screen.

"He's all the way upstairs." Kristen rolled her eyes. "He can't hear pages turning."

"Don't talk back." Ali tossed the video monitor on the glass coffee table. It landed with a loud smash. "Or I'll dock your pay."

"What-*ever*," Kristen mouthed, and then reached for her green glitter binder.

Ali stared at her for an uncomfortable second. "Oh, *I* know what you're smelling." She scooped up a marshmallow with her tongue and mashed it against the roof of her wide mouth.

"What?" Kristen thumbed through her colored divider tabs.

"All that *brown* in your nose."

"Whaddaya mean?"

"I *mean*, who does math homework on New Year's Eve?" she asked, like Jerry Seinfeld doing stand-up.

"People on *scholarships* who need to keep their grades up." Kristen folded her arms across her red Juicy Couture hoodie, the only Christmas gift her parents could afford this year. Not that she'd ever admit *that* to Ali, who only babysat Friday nights to build a résumé for her Ivy League applications. The money was a bonus, a useless prize at the bottom of a cereal box. Her father owned the second-biggest BMW dealership in the tristate area. He hadn't lost his fortune in an art deal gone wrong like Kristen's dad. *She* wasn't living report card to report card, struggling to survive at the most prestigious private school in the county. Hardly. Ali was homeschooled with three other kids from her gated community. They'd have to set her estate on fire to be kicked out.

Ali handed her the Blockbuster box. "Can you *please* try to have some fun?" She tilted her head toward the DVD player, telling Kristen to start the movie. "Besides, classes at OCD don't start for three more weeks."

Kristen looked down at her first pedicure—a holiday gift from her aunt Ginny— and sighed. Would her Baby's Breath Pink toenails still be intact when fourth grade started up again? And if so, would people make fun of her for wearing flip-flops in January? If they even noticed.

It wasn't like she was a loser at Octavian Country Day or anything. In fact, she was the most popular girl on the soccer team. But off the field, when she was in class, Kristen felt like a guest in someone else's home. A very expensive, very exclusive home. A home where no one ate lunch, they *did* lunch. Where Apples were for students, not teachers. Where the letter *A* had more to do with a guest list than a grade. Where Religions were jeans, not beliefs. Where there was no "hip" in *scholarship*.

"Start the movie." Ali nudged Kristen's leg. "Before the Colemans get home. If they open the door while we're watching *Ghost Ship*, we might scream and wake Max."

"Only if you pay me six dollars instead of five," Kristen tried. Not that this job was *completely* about the money. But why not let Ali think that? It was better than the truth: that she didn't have anything better to do.

All the other girls on the soccer team were having a party at the coach's house. But that was two counties over, and Kristen's mother didn't want her so far away on a night when the roads were so full of drunk drivers. As an ER nurse she'd seen, firsthand, what happens to people who get in car accidents on New Year's Eve and said it made roadkill look like rose petals. So it was either babysitting with Ali or hanging out in the condo with Marty, a male nurse from Pediatrics. Kristen chose babysitting.

"Fine, six bucks. Whatever." Ali finger-stirred her Coke.

A buzzing cell phone vibrated across the glass coffee table. In one swift motion, Ali slammed down her soda, lifted her dirty blond hair, and clipped it to the back of her head. She was desperate to protect the blowout she'd gotten from Hair Today, Gone Tomorrow, on the off chance she could make it to her best friend's party before midnight.

"Speak, geek," Ali answered. "What am I missing? Who's there?" She jumped to her feet. "He is? . . . You swear? . . . He *asked* you that? . . ." She leaned against the back of the couch and kicked her legs in the air. "What did you tell him? . . . You did? . . . *Yes!*"

"*Ouuu-wahhhhhhhhh*," cried Max.

"Shhhhhh," Kristen urged smugly.

But Ali kept shouting.

Max got louder.

"Of course I brought a change of clothes. . . . Yeah, the shiny black pair . . . I know, I know. . . . They're perfect." She beamed. "Keep him there as long as possible. I'll try to get out of here before midnight." Ali paused, eyed Kristen, and then hurried toward the kitchen. "She needs the money, what was I supposed to do? Don't worry, I'll send her home first," she whispered. "Okay, cool, I'll check in later. 'Bye." She giggle-snapped her phone shut.

"Ugh, Kristen, what did you do?" Ali hissed, stomping toward the nursery.

Kristen turned on the TV wondering if she should have chosen the pediatric nurse.

Down in New York City, Dick Clark was rockin' Times Square. MTV VJs were counting down the best videos of the year surrounded by midriffs and muscles. CNN was showing celebrations in São Paulo, Brazil. And Merri-Lee

Marvil had commandeered an entire airplane hangar, vacuumed up every red carpet in the country, and dumped the contents on her stage. Four lucky girls in matching Burberry dresses were jumping and cheering while Ricky Martin took the mic. Were they some hot new girl band she'd be hearing about in the New Year? Junior models on assignment for a fashion house? Or maybe they were there solely to remind Kristen how boring and uneventful her existence was, is, and would continue to be, for another three hundred and sixty-five days.

It seemed like everyone in the world was out partying except her and baby Max. Even Ali had plans for later—plans that excluded Kristen.

The Burberry girls threw their arms around each other and shout-sang "She Bangs!"

Kristen clicked on the video monitor. Max was still screaming and Ali was shushing him fervently while applying lip gloss.

Kristen shut off the TV and tossed the remote on the couch. Reflected in the dark screen was a sobering image of herself wearing red sweats and flip-flops, surrounded by textbooks, binders, pencil shavings, and someone else's vibrating phone.

Stepping closer, she looked her reflection in the eye, lifted her right palm, and made her first resolution of the night. "I, Kristen Gregory, promise to do whatever it takes to get a life in the New Year."

Then she kicked her binder off the coffee table and took a long unauthorized swig of Ali's marshmallow Coke. It wasn't exactly life in the fast lane, but at least her pedicured foot was on the gas.

Briiinnnggggggggggggg.

The egg timer rang again.

"Crafts down!" Claire Lyons announced. Her sharply cut New Year's Eve bangs brushed across the tops of her eyebrows while she reset the dial for thirty minutes.

Sarah lowered her glue stick. Sari released her tube of pink glitter. And Mandy placed her paper hat on her lap.

"Is it time already? 'Cause Ifeellikewejustdidthis." Sari stretched out her skinny legs on the white shag rug and began French braiding her long blond hair. Her uncle Bruce had completed his first semester at the Vidal Sassoon Institute and taught her everything he knew about twists over Christmas. There wasn't a doll left in Claire's room whose locks hadn't been woven like challah bread.

"You're right. We did just do this." Claire passed around the silver bowl of gummy worms. "A half hour ago."

"And the half hour before that and the half hour before

that." Mandy picked through the gelatinous tangle until she found three yellows. Her electric blue eyes lit up with joy.

"Sugar is the only way we'll make it to midnight." Claire rolled a new can of grape soda to each girl. "Now drink!" She popped open her Fanta, tilted her head back, and chugged. This was her year. She was finally going to stay awake long enough to see the ball drop. And she was determined to share the moment with her favorite people in the world. Even if it made their teeth rot.

Sarah tilted her head back and yawned. When she straightened up, short butter-yellow curls boinged around her narrow face.

"Only two and a half more hours," Claire urged. She hiked up her plaid flannel Gap pj's and padded over to the Hello Kitty sticker-covered boom box by the bed. "What's that, Britney?" she shouted over "Oops, I Did It Again." "I can't hear you!" She cranked the volume up to nine. "Much better!"

Claire bopped back to the craft circle and happily reclaimed her place on the shag. The girls were making party crowns and masks out of construction paper and metallic markers. They were twisting pipe cleaners into garish jewelry. And salting their hair in their glitter colors—blue for Mandy, pink for Sari, orange for Sarah, and green for Claire. If all went according to plan, and everyone managed to stay awake, they would adorn themselves in their festive creations and pose for a self-timed photo at exactly midnight.

"Ehmagosh, who am I?" Sarah jumped to her feet and hiked up her hearts 'n' bunnies nightgown. She balanced a paper crown on her nest of short blond curls and wobbled across the rug on her tiptoes, smile-waving. Then she tripped and landed on her knees with a thud.

The girls burst out laughing.

"N-n-no." Mandy stood. "It was more like this." She lifted onto her toes, took a few uneven steps, then crashed down on her butt. Strands of damp dark hair covered her pale face.

The CD skipped on the word *ooops*, as if in on the joke.

Sari and Claire joined in, offering their best impressions of the fallen Miss Kiss and the tragic ankle twist that had landed her in the orchestra pit and cost her Kissimmee's most prestigious pageant title. The girls had been imitating her for years. And it never, for one second, stopped being hilarious.

"Watch this one," Sarah shouted, cycloning around the room, her arms spinning at her sides. After eleven dizzying rotations, she stopped and then swayed. Her neck moved like a spring, tipping from side to side under the weight of her woozy head. She teetered stiffly like a zombie on the high seas and then slammed straight into—*thud-smash!*

The Hello Kitty sticker–covered boom box landed on the floor. White plastic splintering across rug was the last sound it ever made.

"What was *that*?" shouted the red-faced teenage babysitter, who, thanks to her prescription zit medication, always looked embarrassed or sunburned. "Is everyone okay?"

"We're fine, Kelsey." Claire sighed at the plastic shards.

"Should I call an ambulance just in case?"

"We're *fine*."

Kelsey surveyed the damage. "Nobody goes near those broken bits, understood?" She tossed a pillow over the crime scene, then jumped back as if it were shooting flames. "I'll be right back with a broom and a—Wait! Where's Todd?"

The girls shrugged.

"Todd?" Kelsey called.

No one answered.

"Todd!" She bolted into the peach carpet–covered hallway and stormed the boy's bedroom next door like a one-woman SWAT team.

"Todd?" she panic-shouted. *"Todd?"* Seconds later, she was back in Claire's room. "Okay, your brother is gone. Totally gone. Was he standing near the boom box when it fell? Did he get hit on the head and wander off in a state of delirium? Oh no. Was the window open?"

Claire and her friends suppressed their giggles. The only thing funnier than Miss Kiss falling into the orchestra pit was watching Kelsey the babysitter panic.

"Oh my heavens, it *was*!" Kelsey stomp-raced over to the window and peered out at the grassy front yard. "Where is he? You can tell me. We don't have to tell your parents if I can confirm his vitals and make sure he's okay."

"I have no clue where he is." Claire rolled her blue eyes, letting her friends know that she was no more okay with Kelsey's intrusion than they were. "Maybe you should check the kitchen or the—"

Ffffffffpuuurpppp. Ffffffffpuuurpppp.

Claire stomped her bare foot. She knew that fake fart sound anywhere. "Todd, come out!" She yelled at her daisy-print comforter.

A shock of orange hair appeared from under the bed. It was attached to a small freckly boy wearing Batman pajamas and a mischievous grin.

"Ehmagosh, was he under there the whole time?" Sari screeched, her thin upper lip practically disappearing from the horror of it all.

Claire responded by shoving Todd out the door. How

would she ever convince her friends to spend New Year's Eve at her house again if they were flanked with a snooping brother and a hyper-protective babysitter?

"It's way past your bedtime, Toddy." Kelsey reached for his hand. "Now, back to night-night for you." She closed the door behind her, purposely leaving it open a crack.

"Now what?" Sari yawned.

Claire checked the timer—nine more minutes until their next sugar hit. "How 'bout a dance contest?' She flicked on her clock radio.

A commercial for Simmons Toyota urged people to drive on down before midnight to take advantage of their crazy year-end deals.

"Let's Google dirty words." Mandy wiggled her thick black eyebrows.

"We did that last Saturday," Sarah whined.

"Well, maybe there are more," Mandy tried. "It's been a week."

Sarah shot her hand in the air. "I know! Let's pretend we're ghosts and scare Kelsey."

Claire giggled at the thought.

Sari and Mandy yanked the white sheet off the twin bed. They gathered underneath in a giddy cluster, bumping into each other and giggling with glee.

"Shhhhhh, listen." Mandy suddenly poked her head out.

"Ffffffffpuuurpppp." Sari did her best impression of Todd's fake fart.

Sarah and Claire cracked up.

"No, seriously." Mandy threw the sheet off their heads. "Turn up the radio."

Claire hurried over to the white Sony Dream Machine and rolled the dial. SCUM 101.1's late-night DJ was playing the Miss Kiss theme song.

"That's right, it's Dr. Party," he announced in the raspy, sleep-deprived voice that had earned him his moniker. "And joining me tonight is the lovely Miss Kiss. Miss Kiss, your reign ends at midnight. How do you feel about that?" He made a crude sniffing sound. "By the way, has anyone ever told you you smell like grapefruit?"

She giggled. "It's Happy, by Clinique. One of the wonderful sponsors I had the opportunity to work with over the past year."

"Well, it's making *me* happy, I'll tell you that." Dr. Party chuckled like a perv.

The girls rolled their eyes.

Miss Kiss giggled again. "Sorry, what did you ask me?" Her high-pitched voice sounded slightly muffled, like she was curling up shyly and speaking into her shoulder.

"Are you going to miss Miss Kiss?"

"Oh yeah," she said, suddenly sounding serious and

rehearsed. "I'm going to miss it so much. I've gotten to work with so many wonderful people, charities, and mammals. And I learned bunches about all the different car shows in the state of Florida. Did you know there are over nineteen different exhibitions on the Gulf Coast alone? And that doesn't include antique shows or monster trucks."

"We have to take another break, but for those of you dying to get a whiff of this lovely lady beside me, be the first caller to properly name the last five Kissimmee pageant winners. If you can, you and Miss Kiss will ride in our station limo to see tonight's midnight performance of Orlando's very own boy band, ThRob, at Disney's Grand Floridian Resort and Spa. Their song 'Twice the Fun' will be broadcast live via satellite on Merri-Lee Marvil's *New Year's Yves*. And so will *you*, when twins Theo and Rob plant a big smooch on your lips, making you their first kiss of the New Year. And you know what they say? You never forget your first, right?" He snorted, making Trojan, his sidekick, cackle-cough. "Phone lines are open. The number to dial is 1-800-YRU-SCUM. That's 1-800-YRU-SCUM. Back in a flash with Dr. Party and Trojan on Florida's destination station, SCUM 101.1."

"Ahhhhhhhh!" The girls scrambled for their Nokias.

Claire, who had been forbidden to get a cell phone until her sixteenth birthday, ran into her parents' bedroom and grabbed the tan cordless off the cradle. She dialed and immediately got through. Her insides soared. Finally, a New Year's Eve worth remembering. "I'm in," she shouted-ran back to her room, forgetting all about Kelsey and her sleeping brother.

"Me too." Mandy sucked on a piece of black hair.

"Same." Sarah bounced on her toes.

"Number three!" Sari announced.

Mandy and Sarah immediately ended their calls.

"Why'dya do *that*?" Claire gasped.

"I had number fifty-nine." Mandy sighed.

"Sixty-one." Sarah moped.

An automated voice informed Claire that she was eighty-seventh in line.

"How did you get so close?" Claire asked Sari, hanging up.

"I have them on speed-dial," confessed the bony blond. "For All-Request Wednesdays."

"Dr. Party and Trojan, back with the lovely Miss Kiss during her last moments as our reigning hottie."

She tee-heed at the compliment.

"Time to turn to the phones and find some lips for Theo and Rob, the twin brothers in ThRob, to kiss at midnight. Caller one, can I have your name please?"

"Theo and Rob can kiss my pimple-infested a—"

Dr. Party disconnected the line with an embarrassed

chuckle. "Next caller. Can you name the last five winners of the Miss Kiss pageant?"

"Oh my lord, Dr. Party, is that really you? I swear I'm a huge fan. I saw you perform at the Comedy Castle last month and you were hair-sterical!"

"Thank you, uh . . ."

"Jillian!"

"Jillian. Okay, Jillian. Can you name the last five Miss Kisses?"

Claire, Sarah, Sari, and Mandy gripped hands and shook their heads, cosmically jinxing Jillian.

"I sure can. Polly Cayman . . ."

No more.

"Vicki Tomlinson . . ."

No! Stop!

"Camille Anning . . ."

JINX! Double jinx! Triple jinx!!!!

Claire's palms began to sweat. She felt like she was being robbed.

"Hayden Henning . . ."

"Yes!" Claire pulled her hand away from Sari's and punched the air with joy.

"Awww, so close." Dr. Party sounded genuinely upset as he hung up on Jillian. And then, with a quick click, he was on to the next caller. "You're on with SCUM 101.1, can I have your name, please?"

No one responded. "Number three, can I have your name please?" The only sound he got was the deafening screech of feedback. "Caller number three, turn off your radio and—"

"Ehmagosh, caller three!" Claire shouted at Sari.

The girl was statue-still.

"Stage fright!" Mandy barked. "Someone grab it!

Sarah backed away.

Without thinking, Claire yanked the phone away from Sari's ear and turned off her Dream Machine. "Hi, Dr. Party, this is Claire."

"Hi, Claire, can you—"

"PollyCaymanVickiTomlinsonCamilleAnningJenni EaganandCoraShandler. Hayden Henning was the original winner but she fell during her acceptance walk and the crown was given to Jenni."

A cheering-crowd sound effect blasted in the background. Claire's friends fused together in a victorious group hug.

"Stay on the line, Claire, so we can get your address," Dr. Party told her. "A limo is on the way!"

"Ahhhhhhhh!" The girls began screaming and jumping.

"What are we going to wear?" asked Sarah, wiggling out of her pj's.

"Nothing!" Sari joked, whipping off her nightgown.

They stomped on their paper hats and masks in a mad dash for the closet.

"Shhhh." Claire pointed to the open bedroom door.

"How are we going to get past Kelsey?" Mandy whispered, wrapping an old orange and black Halloween boa around her neck.

"Very quietly," whispered Claire, dabbing her lips with green glitter. "Very, *very* quietly."

With the help of a huffy security guard and a keen eye for "fashion don'ts," Massie found her way back to the Ahnnabees. They were standing in the center of the crowd, sipping smoothies out of champagne flutes. It was obvious from the four half-empty tumblers by their feet, and the pink stain down the middle of Brianna's Burberry, that they had transferred the drinks into the grown-up glasses themselves. As if *flutes* would somehow fool people into thinking they had style.

"What happened to you?" Ahnna asked, placing a sticky palm on Massie's shoulder. "We were soooo worried."

Lana, Brianna, and Shauna nodded slowly in agreement, their lips assuming various interpretations of a concerned pout.

"You were?" Massie squinted, trying to spot the truth. Her insides felt like a soft-serve vanilla-chocolate ice cream cone—half light, half dark. A swirling blend of wanting to believe Ahnna and not trusting her.

"Of *course* we were." Anna smiled slowly, baring her

oversize front teeth. "You weren't here for the check-in call with my dad. And he was mad. He said if anyone's missing for the next check-in he'll take us home. Midnight or *not*!"

"And that makes us worried," Lana added, a thin blue vein bulging in her neck.

"*Very* worried." Shauna took off her red glasses and glared.

"Very, *ver*—"

"I get it!" Massie snapped, cutting Brianna off. "But if you hadn't run off like that I never would have gotten lost and—"

"*Who's gonna show me their thong?*" shouted a deep voice over the microphone.

"Whooooooooooooo!" answered the audience.

All of a sudden, a lively, booty-shaking beat filled the hangar.

"Let me see that thonnnnng," the voice began singing a cappella.

More cheering.

And then, a bare-chested muscular man in baggy white pants flipped onto the stage. His dark skin had been shined to reflect the pulsating stage lights.

"Sisqó!" Ahnna shouted. She quickly placed her champagne flute on the floor in preparation to rush the stage. The other Ahnnabees did the same.

Massie looked around, wondering if anyone had a problem with four girls leaving eight fragile glasses on a packed dance floor. But no one seemed to notice. All anyone cared about was shaking their backsides and—

"Ehmagawd, stawp!" Massie shouted. "I see Her!"

Her being short for Hermia, Merri-Lee's infamous resident psychic.

But the girls had already made a break for the stage.

"I said, stop!" she shouted louder.

Several models, barely wider than the straws in their fruity cocktails, froze mid-grind.

"No, not you." Massie blushed. *"Them!"*

"Who? Za Good, Za Plaid, and Za Ugly?" joked an exotic blonde wearing a white thigh-dusting dress. Her date's necktie hung sloppily around her neck.

Massie giggle-nodded. *Not a bad joke for a model.*

She raced to catch up with Ahnna, then tapped her on the shoulder.

"That thong th-thong thong thong!" Ahnna gyrated-sang as she whipped her head around to face Massie. *"What?"*

"Hermia's *here*!" Massie pointed to the gold tent at the edge of the dance floor.

"I can read," Ahnna snapped. Her heavily lined brown eyes fixed on the video screen beside the tent. The spiritual messenger's face—spackled with makeup and framed by a mass of ruby red hair—appeared alongside footage of the earthquakes, stock market fluctuations, and celebrity breakups that had occurred in the past year. All of which Hermia had predicted. *The future is coming. Are you ready?* appeared in spooky black calligraphy with a massive digital clock counting down the hours, minutes, and seconds until the New Year. The phrase pulsated on-screen and then vanished.

"We *have* to see her," Massie urged. "We can find out if LMNOP will—"

"How 'bout we show Sisqó some love!" Merri-Lee cooed into the mic from the dancers' pit at the bottom of the stage, her red hair radiating a fresh dye job. It was the first time Massie had ever seen her in person. And if she could get close enough, she might advise her to go lighter on the blush. "How much do we love him?"

The hangar echoed with a torrent of eager applause. "And now, coming to you via satellite from Orlando, the boy-band capital of the world, please welcome one of this year's hottest groups, N'S—"

"Eeeeeeeeeeeeeeee!" The Ahnnabees shook their hands and ran-shoved to the front of the stage.

"They're nawt even here!" Massie called after them. "It's via satellite!"

But that obviously didn't matter. In a blur of Bur, the Ahnnabees were gone.

An itchy wool peacoat of sadness hung over Massie's entire body, weighing her down with despair. She'd ditched her parents, Paris, and Chanel shopping for *this*? Not even one compliment on her fetching outfit/chignon/makeup/charm bracelet/brooches/or ability to pull off mixed metals had come her way. *Nawt one!*

It was only a matter of time before people started to stare. Not because of her fetching outfit/chignon/makeup/charm bracelet/brooches/ability to pull off mixed metals. But because she was standing in the middle of a thumping dance floor on New Year's Eve at the best party in the country, motionless, friendless, and on the verge of tears.

A camera on tracks rolled by. What if someone saw her on TV? *Alone?*

Out of sheer desperation, Massie flipped open her cell and managed a half-smile. The only way to save pride was to fake a phoner and get out of there. *Fast.*

"Heyyyy." She burst out laughing as if Jim Carrey was on the other end. "What? . . . No! . . . Did you say private jet or private *fete*? Seriously? . . . Wait, I can't hear you. . . . Hold awn. . . ." She jammed a finger in her ear, then marched toward the gold tent, like whatever Jim was saying was urgent, possibly tragic, and deserved her undivided attention.

A snaking line of women, some glossing, others biting their nails, most drinking pink cocktails, had formed outside Hermia's lair.

Massie's glossy lips began to quiver. The only thing worse than being solo in the middle of a dance floor was standing at the back of a line on New Year's Eve to see a TV psychic. Little said *I am beyond miserable and need hope* quite like that. Tears were on the way, and they were bringing friends. Massie hurried toward the tent flaps.

Just as she was about to enter, a heavy hand descended on her shoulder, its square fingernails digging into her flesh. "Back it up, honey. We've been standing on this line since last New Year's. No cutting!"

You talking to me or your manicurist, Clawberry Shortcake?

Turning slowly, Massie sniffled. "I wasn't *cutting*." She locked eyes with her captor and then released the first teardrop. "I—I need to see my mommy. It's an emergency."

"Jenna's not your *mommy*," the woman slurred.

"She's not even married," added her friend. She tucked a frosted curl behind her ruby-studded ear. "Or dating for that matter."

"Hasn't had a guy for years, thanks to Rick," said Clawberry. "That's why she's with *Her*."

They burst out laughing.

"Nawt Jenna." Massie wiped her salt-stained cheek. *"Hermia."*

"Hermia's your *mother*?"

Massie nodded. Clawberry released her grip. "You are so lucky. You must always know—"

"Yip." Massie rolled her eyes, feigning boredom with her mother's *gift*, and then hurried inside.

"Um, excuse me." A red-nosed woman, probably Jenna, blew into a tissue. "This is *my* reading."

"I know, but your friends wanted me to tell you Rick is here," Massie said with an innocent grin. "I think that's what they said. Rick or Ray or something?"

"Really?" Jenna sniffed back years of heartache and rolled her shoulders. Her face seemed to change from black-and-white to color, like Dorothy when she landed in Oz.

Jenna leaned over the table of tarot cards and gave the psychic a condescending squeeze. "Nice try, Hermia. But you were wrong. He left his wife! He left her! I knew he would. I *knew* it!"

Hermia smiled with her mouth pressed shut.

"Thank you!" Jenna kissed Massie on the cheek, grabbed her black sequin clutch, and bolted.

"Yes?" Hermia asked, her tone dripping suspicion. "And how can I help you, Ms.? . . ."

Um, shouldn't you know?

"Block. Massie Block." She helped herself to a seat on the vacant but still warm wood stool.

Around her, the tent was ripe with the smell of dust and chai. Piles of Moroccan pillows, overlapping Oriental rugs, and the warm glow of candlelight surrounded Massie like an exotic womb. Beyond the gold velvet walls, the party was in full swing; staccato bursts of laughter, bass booming from the speakers, clinking crystal. . . . Yet everything was muffled like the distant dinner party noises that often lulled Massie to sleep while her parents entertained. They were the sounds of feeling safe.

Hermia crossed her fleshy arms over her maroon-colored caftan and glared at Massie expectantly, as if she'd just powered up a cell phone and was waiting for a signal.

"What?" Massie giggled and anxiously crossed her legs.

Hermia held out her palm—a map of cracks and lines that were tinted orange. (Henna? Spray tan? Beta-carotene poisoning?) Without hesitation Massie offered her hand. Her charm bracelet fell over her thumb. "Sorry," she said shyly. "It's a little loose."

Hermia grinned patiently.

"I'm not really sure why I'm here," she began nervously. "I just needed a place to—"

"No more," Hermia insisted, closing her gold-shadowed lids and tossing back her flaming red hair. She rocked back and forth and exhaled with dragonlike force—and then began to chant: "*Spiritus maximus shareshareshare . . . spiritus maximus shareshareshare . . . spiritus maximus share-shareshare . . .*"

Massie bit her lower lip to keep from giggling. Was this funny or creepy? Gawd, if only her friends were there she wouldn't feel so awkward . . . pathetic . . . terrified!

"*. . . spiritus maximus shareshareshare spiritus maximus shareshareshare spiritus maximus shareshareshare spiritus maximus sh—*"

Suddenly, Hermia's wrinkled lids popped open. In a deep, hushed voice, which seemed on loan from someone more serious, she began. "As always, you are at the *it* party. With the *it* crowd. Wearing the *it* wardrobe. But you just aren't feeling . . . eh . . . I don't know. . . ." She closed her eyes and moved them back and forth, like she was reading something inside her head. "*It!* You just aren't feeling *it!* Am I right?"

"Yes!" Massie's stomach lurched. Hermia was *so* right! All her life she'd felt detached, like she was being massaged in a snowsuit. And it was time for that snowsuit to come off.

"You have surrounded yourself with the wrong people," Hermia continued.

Massie nodded in agreement, her palm soaking with sweat. Was it time for the snowsuit to come off?

"You are a girl of many ideas. Strong ideas. Gooood ideas. But you are not being heard."

"Ah-greed!" Massie shouted. It wasn't enough anymore to *believe* she was *it*. She wanted to *feel* it. And she wanted to *feel it now*!

"You were born to lead, not follow."

"Yes! Yes!"

"But you must gather your power first," Hermia insisted. "Draw it to you. Be a human magnet. Attract the necessary pieces."

"Huh?"

"When all five pieces are together, you will reach your full potential as a leader."

"What *pieces*?" Massie snapped. Did she have to be so ah-nnoyingly mysterious? What did that mean? Why couldn't Hermia just *tell* her what to do?

Massie opened her clutch and pulled out a crisp twenty. "What if I give you this? Will you tell me what the pieces are?"

The psychic released Massie's hand. "Hermia cannot be bought!"

Massie rolled her eyes and stood. She'd gotten what she came for. She was going to be the leader of the Ahn-nabees. That was all she needed to know.

"Wait!" Hermia held out a smooth purple stone. "Take this. It's *free*." She smirked.

"What's it for?"

"Purple is the color of royalty, you know. And that's the color I see when I look at you."

"Ehmagawd, me *too*." Massie reached for the stone. It would look adorable in her future crown.

```
┌─────────────────────────────────────────────┐
│                                               │
│   MERRI-LEE MARVIL'S NEW YEAR'S YVES PARTY    │
│              DRESSING ROOM C                  │
│           Friday, December 31st               │
│                8:41 P.M.                      │
│                                               │
└─────────────────────────────────────────────┘
```

Thirty-four minutes until curtain.

Alicia speed mashed a not-quite-ripe banana with a plastic fork. The white prongs bent against what was supposed to be the planet's softest fruit. But tough banana and brown rice would have to do. They were the only options on the "performers' food table" reputed for intestinal binding. And Andrea's intestines needed some serious binding.

"Is Mrs. Fossier back yet?" Andrea moaned.

"She's searching for ginger ale." Alicia crouched down beside the couch and offered up a forkful of banan-ice. "Eat!"

"Ew." Brooke winced from across the room. "That *looks* like the stuff you're trying to get rid of."

"Ugggghhhhh." Andrea curled into fetal position and turned away, her gas-leaking butt aiming straight for Alicia's face.

"Brooke, do you *mind*?" Alicia hissed. "We have twenty-five minutes to find a cure for And-rrhea or we're going to be replaced by singing dogs."

"Ha! And-rrhea!" Brooke burst out laughing. "That's a good one."

Alicia allowed herself a quick giggle. "Eat!"

Andrea popped open the snap on her pin-striped shorts and cupped her distended belly. "I can't. You'll have to find someone else to dance." A fresh set of hives marred her neck.

"You're right," Alicia sighed, wondering what Skye would do in this situation. Would she replace Andrea? Force-feed her the banan-ice? Or would everything have been fine had Skye been here? What if this "nerve problem" was a reaction to Alicia? What if Alicia's captaining was making Andrea sick?

Considering this made Alicia's stomach plunge. She was so close to being number one. And as usual, someone was getting in her way.

A muffled ringing sound drew her back. It was coming from the bottom of her new caramel-colored Marc Jacobs tote. *Thanks, Santa!*

Whoever was calling would have to wait. She was in crisis mode. This was no time to discuss celeb sightings with the couch-ridden girls in her grade.

But the caller kept calling. And calling. And . . .

With a frustrated sigh Alicia dug deep into her MJ. She dug beyond the Juicy sweats. Beyond the hair products. Beyond the sealed box of Nair. And pulled out her pink Nokia.

The display flashed SKYE HAMILTON.

Ehmagawd, was she back? Did her Hawaii trip get canceled? Was she ready to dance? Could she be here in twenty minutes? Normally Alicia would have ignored the bossy captain, but under the circumstances, she would gladly welcome her back.

"*Skye!*" she answered, sounding slightly out of breath. "Hey! Are you ba—"

"What did you do to Andrea? Why is she so nervous? Do you realize how important this night is? Not only for the troupe but for my parents' studio?" She continued screaming but Alicia tuned her out. Instead she covered the mouthpiece and whispered to Andrea. "Did you call her?"

Andrea bit her bottom lip and nodded yes, like a child caught drawing on the furniture.

Alicia's heart tapped like Riverdance.

How *dare* And-rrhea undermine her authority by calling Skye in Hawaii!

How dare Skye blame her for And-rrhea's nerves!

How dare Brooke sit so peacefully in the corner, bopping her head to some peppy song while Alicia's world fell apart?

How dare Mrs. Fossier disappear on a ginger ale hunt instead of trying to find a new dancer?

She turned to the wall-mounted TV monitor above her head. The audience was applauding like crazy.

Sisqó was ending his performance and leading his backup dancers off the stage. The last one, an Asian beauty, couldn't have been all that much older than Alicia. And she was dancing for one of the biggest rap stars of the year. *It wasn't fair!* Alicia was just as good as she was. But no one would ever know. Because her one big shot—*Ehmagawd!*

"That's it!" Alicia pressed her French-manicured thumbnail into the end button. She grabbed her tote, marched toward the door, and threw it open.

"Where are you going?" Brooke shouted over the music in her earbuds.

But Alicia didn't bother answering. She didn't have time.

Outside the dressing room, the halls were crackling with energy. Costumed performers and frenzied stage managers hurried by like schools of fish. But Alicia swam upstream, fighting the crowd, determined to find . . . *There she was!*

The girl was even prettier in person. She had short black bangs and a long ponytail that was so shiny it looked wet. Her mouth was a perfect circle and her puffy lips were stained pink. Her body was more muscular than Alicia's and her boobs were smaller. If Alicia hadn't been so desperate she would have dismissed the girl for being too pretty to perform with. This was like a shadow asking to dance with a light. She was sure to fade next to the beauty. But at least the shadow would be on national TV. Once it was over, Alicia could get a copy of the performance and have the girl edited out. If Mariah Carey could have her torso digitally stretched in her videos, surely something could be done to make Alicia a solo star.

"'Scuse me," Alicia said in her most confident voice. It was important the girl know she was an equal and not a fan. "I'm Alicia. And you are?"

"Poppy." The dancer raised one of her thin brows and puckered her lips. It was the classic *speak—I'm waiting* pose. Alicia had perfected it back in the third grade.

"I'll give you two hundred dollars if you dance for me." Alicia tapped the soft caramel leather tote.

"I am *not* that kind of dancer," Poppy hissed.

"Huh?" Alicia asked, before understanding the misunderstanding. "*Ew!* I didn't mean it like that! I'm captain of BADSS." She paused, giving the girl a chance to gush about how she'd heard of them. But her *speak—I'm waiting* pose was all she offered.

"One of my girls is sick and I need a replacement. You seem decent enough and you're the right size for the costume, so—"

"Is *that* the costume?" Poppy cocked her head, scanning the silver sequin–covered tuxedo vest and pinstriped short shorts.

"Everything except the leg warmers," Alicia said proudly. "They're captain-only."

"I dunno." Poppy scrunched her lips as if trying to sniff her own gloss.

"Puh-lease! It's much more *modern* than what you're wearing," Alicia said to Poppy's ripped denim shorts and black demi-cup bra. "At least my costume comes with a *shirt*."

"Then you and your *shirt* should go find a nice mirror to dance in front of because it's the only way you're ever gonna—"

"Okay, wait!" Alicia grabbed the girl's boy-arm. "I'll give you three hundred dollars."

"Hmmmmm . . ." Poppy folded her arms across her bra while she considered this.

Alicia tapped her foot impatiently. "Hurry. I still have to teach you the routine and—"

"Fine." Poppy smiled at a passing dancer. "On one condition."

"Anything." Alicia's shoulders softened.

"The bag."

"Huh?" Alicia's armpit pressed a little harder against the braided strap.

"I want your bag."

"No way! I just got it for Christmas!"

Instantly, Poppy turned away. Her ponytail swung

with such sass Alicia could practically hear it say, *See ya, sucker!*

"Fine! Have it!"

Poppy returned and reached for her prize.

Alicia took a quick step back. "*After* we dance." She squeezed the margarine-soft leather, assuring it that the decision was nothing personal. Just business.

Show business.

Limo lights streaked across Claire's bedroom walls, prison watchtower style.

"*It's time!*" she whisper-commanded, poking her face into the hallway. "Remember, it's all about speed and silence. We have to get to that driver before he rings the bell."

The girls nodded dutifully, then followed her down the peach-carpeted stairs.

At the landing, Claire held out her palm like a crossing guard, urging them to stop while she checked the perimeter. Images from the muted TV flickered against the recliners, glass coffee table, and half-empty pizza box as if Martians had abducted Kelsey.

If only! Claire sighed.

She was probably in the bathroom, smacking more Silly Putty–colored cover-up on her benzoyl-peroxided cheeks, or making sure the childproof caps were engaged on the medicine bottles, just in case someone decided to sleepwalk with their mouth open.

It was now or never.

Sarah, Sari, and Mandy huddled close on the bottom

step, each dressed in one of Claire's old theater costumes. They looked like a nervous tween act about to take the stage in a local talent competition.

As escape missions went, this was no *Shawshank*. There was no exit strategy. No plan for reentry. And no *way* Claire's parents would forgive her if she got caught. Still, she had to try. Because turning down a shot at a New Year's Eve kiss from ThRob would be like Cinderella refusing to try on the glass slipper because it hadn't been properly sanitized. If you want to be swept off your feet, you have to be prepared to fall—and then hope like hot dogs you don't.

"*Now!*" mouthed Claire, lifting the stiff red chiffon hem of her Scarlett O'Hara dress.

In a rush of glitter, tulle, and tassels, the girls tiptoed toward the front door. Cracking it open with no more than a tiny kiss sound, Claire smiled back at her friends. They were free!

All of a sudden, a bright light smacked Claire in the eyes. A microphone was thrust in her face. And a woman began to speak.

"Meet Claire Lyons, the girl chosen by SCUM 101.1 to kiss Orlando's very own ThRob at midnight."

Claire giggled awkwardly. What was happening? Was this the news? *America's Most Wanted*?

"Are you a ThRob fan, Claire?"

She giggled again, and then quickly warmed to the

attention. *"Totally."* She beamed, feeling the weight of her friends pressing against her back.

"Heyyyy!" They waved into the camera.

"What's *this*?" screeched a familiar voice. Without turning, Claire knew it was Kelsey. "Get in the house! Now!" She grabbed each of the girls by the backs of their costumes, pulled them inside, and slammed the door in the reporter's face. "You're in huge trouble," Kelsey barked. "Huge!"

The words coiled around Claire's body and squeezed out all her joy.

"I had no idea they were there," she tried to explain, her hands still a shaking mix of excitement and fear.

"I had no idea *you* were there." Kelsey chewed her bottom lip until it was redder than her cheeks. "Would someone care to explain?"

"Run!" Sarah made a break for the door, a flurry of yellow and black glitter falling from her costume and forming a mini glitter puddle on the carpet.

Kelsey blocked her with a stiff arm to the chest. "What's with the bumblebee?"

"I told you I looked like a *bee*!" Sarah pouted.

"Well, it *is* a bee costume," Mandy explained.

"Easy for you to say!" Sarah's blond curls bounced indignantly. "You got the Princess Fiona gown."

"At least you're not in a blue romper," Sari chimed in,

tugging at her Dorothy dress. "Claire, why couldn't you have been a model instead of an actress? The clothes would be way cool—"

"Silence!" Kelsey brandished a tan cordless phone like a sword. "I want Mr. and Mrs. Lyons to hear me *clearly* when I tell them you were sneaking out to be on some reality show." She began dialing.

"*Reality* show?" Mandy giggled.

"Wait!" Claire reached for the phone.

Kelsey pulled it back.

The limo horn honked.

"Who is *that*?" Kelsey pushed past the girls and stepped outside. A chill filled the front foyer.

"Kelsey, wait!" Claire tugged the bottom of the baby-sitter's lavender crewneck. "You don't understand!"

"No, *you* don't understand." She smacked Claire's hand away. "I had to combine all my holiday gift cards to buy this J. Crew sweater. It's a wool and cashmere blend. Stretch it and *cry*."

"But just listen," Claire pleaded.

"Yeah, Kelsey, just listen." Sari stomped her ruby red–slippered foot.

The others nodded with urgency.

Kelsey ignored them and stepped farther out onto the front porch. "Go home!" she shouted, waving the driver off. "No thank you!"

"Kelsey, *wait*!" Claire begged.

"We're not interested!" she continued. "Not interested!"

The driver started the engine.

"No, *wait*!" Claire called. But it was too late. The limo rolled down the street like a rejected boy at a dance.

"How could you do this to me?" Claire cried. Her night was ruined. Her New Year's Eve was ruined. Her life was ruined. "This doesn't just happen every day, you *know*?" she sobbed, not caring if her friends were watching. Not caring if the neighbors could hear. Not caring that the babysitter had no clue what she was talking about.

Kelsey slammed the door.

"What doesn't happen every day? You sneaking out of your house? You being totally irresponsible? You—"

"Kelsey?" chirped a familiar voice from the living room.

"Todd!" Claire stomped her navy Keds sneaker. "Stay out of this!"

"But I have a question." The little redhead emerged from behind the La-Z-Boy. "What does *irresponsible* mean?" He curl-buried his fists inside the sleeves of his Batman pj's.

"Toh-odd!" Claire sniffled. "Just go to bed, okay?"

Kelsey held up her pinkish palm. "It's okay, Claire. He can learn from this. I'll allow it."

Todd beamed smugly.

The babysitter crouched down and met Todd's brown

eyes. "Irresponsible means, hmmmm, let me see, how can I explain it? . . ." She scanned the stucco ceiling until . . . "Okay, ir-re-sponsible means breaking the rules when people trusted you to follow them." She gripped his narrow shoulders. "An example would be: Claire and her friends were irresponsible when they tried to sneak out of the house. Or, Claire's parents will say she was irresponsible and that's why they are going to ground her. "

Todd smiled. "Oh, I get it."

"Good." Kelsey stood, then dusted off her jeans like she had just fixed a leaking sink.

Claire met her friends' eyes and silently apologized for what was turning out to be the worst New Year's Eve ever. They responded by looking away. The international sign for *you are too pathetic to make eye contact with*.

"Is this right?" Todd put his hands on his hips like a superhero. "Kelsey is ir-re-sponsible because her boyfriend is hiding in the broom closet."

"*What?*" the babysitter snapped.

"Or how about, Kelsey is ir-re-sponsible because Mr. and Mrs. Lyons told her no friends or boys while she's working and she's broken that rule almost every Friday for the last year."

The invisible joy-sucking coil released its grip around Claire. Her tears dried like puddles after a sun shower.

Her love for Todd ran deeper than a groundhog. "There's a *boy* in here?"

Todd wagged his thumb toward the kitchen.

Sarah, Sari, and Mandy shriek-ran toward the mystery guest.

"Wait!" Kelsey called, chasing after them. But she was too slow. The girls ripped open the narrow door and shrieked.

There stood a very embarrassed strawberry blond boy with the physique of a bendy straw—thin and arched. His cheeks were flushed. And his black sweatshirt and skinny gray jeans were covered in dust bunnies. "Hey," he croaked.

"This is Zadrienne," Todd announced. "His real name is *Adrienne*." He giggled. "Adrienne, like a *girl*." He giggled again. "He told Kelsey he changed his name last week. After they kissed. On the lips!" He turned bright red. "I saw it. It was grosser than spaghetti barf."

"You've been *spying* on us?" Kelsey's heart-shaped mouth fell open. She fanned her reddening cheeks and leaned against the kitchen table for support.

"You said he was *asleep*!" Zadrienne smacked his shiny forehead.

"I thought he *was*!"

Claire stood back and grinned. "My parents are not gonna like this."

Kelsey's head tilted left—a silent plea for mercy.

Claire giggled. Like her father always said, things had a funny way of working out. "Unless . . ."

"What?" Kelsey asked, biting her thumbnail.

"How did Adrienne get here?"

"Zayyyy-drienne," he corrected.

The girls giggled.

"Whatever, how did he get here?"

"He drove," Kelsey offered.

"Drove *what*?" Claire began pacing like a frustrated interrogator.

"His Prius."

"Kels, I better get going." Zadrienne saluted, then hurried toward the side door. "I'll call you later."

"Wait!" Claire insisted with a swoosh of her Scarlett O'Hara dress.

Sarah, Sari, and Mandy air-clapped in anticipation.

"If you drive us to the Disney's Grand Floridian Resort and Spa, wait with us until midnight, then drive us home, I'll keep your secret."

Zadrienne opened his mouth in protest, revealing two rows of silver braces.

"And if you don't," Claire continued, "I'll make my parents fire Kelsey and arrest you for trespassing."

The girls bounced with glee. Claire wanted to join them but forced herself to remain stern. There would be plenty of time for celebrating later.

"Zadrienne?" Kelsey pressed her dusty boyfriend for an answer.

"I don't have enough gas," he tried.

"Aren't those things electric?" Mandy added.

"No!" he snapped. "Besides, I promised my sister she could have it by eleven."

"Better un-promise," Sari hissed, her upper lip curling into obscurity.

Claire fought the urge to high-five her.

"Come on, Zay!" Kelsey pleaded.

He sighed. "Fine."

"Yeahhhhhhhhhhhh!" The girls came together and hug-squealed for joy.

Minutes later, a bitter babysitter, her soon-to-be ex-boyfriend, Scarlett O'Hara, Batman, Princess Fiona, and a bumblebee were jam-packed in a little red Prius—heading for lights, cameras, and plenty of action.

Navigating the packed dance floor felt different now. Glares and glances no longer felt like judgments. They felt like pleas for acceptance—as if these people suddenly knew that Massie was the keeper of the purple stone. That she was destined to be the leader of something big, and that she would get right to it as soon as Blink 182 finished playing "What's My Age Again." Even the band seemed to know that Ahnna's reign was more done than disco.

That's about the time she broke up with me,
No one should take themselves so seriously . . .

Massie winked *thank you* to Mark Hoppus while he was singing. And from where she was standing, it looked like he winked back *you deserve this*. And with that, Massie pushed through the crowd with renewed force. Her shoves no longer said, *Um, could you please make room? . . . Mind the toes. . . . Please don't trample me. . . .* They said, *Move! Do you know who I am? I said, MOVE!*

The Burberry Bunch were at the front of the stage, right where she left them. Their foreheads were slick with sweat, their voices hoarse from screaming, and their pits ripe with the smell of Funyuns.

No one acknowledged Massie when she joined their dance cluster. Had they even noticed she was gone? She reached inside the pocket of her dress and rubbed her thumb against the cool flat surface of the stone, releasing more of its power. Then she rubbed it again. And again . . .

She needed all the help she could get. . . .

The performance ended with a final bang of the drums.

"Where *were* you?" Ahnna snapped.

Massie grinned. Her days of answering to Ahnna were almost over.

"Stawp smiling, it's not funny." Ahnna peeled some sweat-stuck curls off her forehead. "Since *your* parents didn't want to spend New Year's Eve with you, *my* parents are responsible . . ."

Owie.

". . . and they wanted another head count." She paused dramatically. "I had to lie, Massie. *Lie!* Why? Because *you* were gone. Ah-*gain*! Do you know how that made me *feel*?"

"Like you're losing friends?" Massie asked, stone-faced.

Shauna, Brianna, and Lana gasped then giggled. Massie saw a glimpse of her future . . . a future with Friday night sleepovers, wardrobe summits, Isaac-driven mall trips, and a royal purple bedroom. . . .

"How am *I* losing friends?" Ahnna's brown eyes bulged.

Massie stood firm, despite the stream of people pushing their way to the bar before the next performance. "Because I have all the power now," she bellowed, feeling like Moses in that old movie *The Ten Commandments*.

"*What?*" Ahnna practically snorted. She made a goofy face at the other girls, implying Massie was crazy.

They goofied back in agreement.

Massie turned to Hermia's tent, like it was a customer-service help line and she had a faulty product. Perhaps Hermia could offer a few tips on how this transfer of power might go down. But the only thing Massie got was the sudden urge to end this drama and get on with the rest of her royal life.

"This means I have the power now. Just accept it." She pinched the stone between her thumb and index finger and held it under Ahnna's pert nose.

"Stawp!" Ahnna whacked Massie's arm away from her face.

The gold charm bracelet flew off Massie's wrist and landed by Lana's foot. The lanky brunette scooped it up and let it dangle between Massie and Ahnna, unsure of whom to give it to. "Here you go," she finally said, obviously hoping someone would take it.

But Massie couldn't move. She was frozen by the realization that she'd just let some celebrity psychic lead her to revolution without a plan, an army, or a chance. Her destiny had never been clearer. Or more grim.

"The only thing I'm going to *accept*," Ahnna finally responded, "is that your Cracker Jack bracelet is too cheap to stay on your bony wrist." She grabbed it from Lana and began twirling it around her finger. "Maybe my little sister can use it. She's always losing the pieces to our Monopoly game."

Massie recalled the joy in her parents' voices when they'd presented her with the bracelet. She pictured Inez outside her door grinning because she'd made it up the stairs in time for the surprise. Then she remembered the Ahnnabees' envious expressions when they first saw the trendsetting piece. And she knew. The bracelet was special. It was more than an accessory. Each charm represented part of her soul. And her soul was worth fighting for.

"Give it back!" Massie swiped like a frisky cat, hooking her finger around the gold chain.

Grinning, Ahnna pulled it back.

Scowling, Massie pulled it forward.

Squinting, Ahnna pulled it back.

Grunting, Massie pulled it forward.

Wincing, Ahnna pulled it back.

And then—*pppsht!*—it was gone. The chain broke in two and the charms scatter-bounced across the stiletto-stabbed concrete like spilled Tic Tacs and disappeared.

Ahnna-you-dizn't!

Forgetting her pride, her dress, her bare knees, and the densely packed dance floor, Massie dropped to the ground. The house DJ began playing "Gone" by N'Sync and the stilettos began to stomp.

On all fours, palming the floor amidst a barrage of spiked heels was so *nawt* how she wanted to ring in the New Year. Not even close.

"Will someone please *help*?" Massie shouted up at the Ahnnabees.

A college-age hipster in a brown leather suit and white Converse high-tops extended his hand. "You hurt?"

Massie looked up at his warm smile and teared. "No." She lowered her head, "'M okay."

Finally, Lana and Shauna dropped to their knees. Brianna stood by Ahnna and glared, their faces bloated with superiority.

"How many are we looking for?' Lana asked, like maybe she actually cared.

"Five," Massie sniffled, her knees pressing into the cold concrete while everyone above her danced. How would she ever find five charms in this mess of heels and—"Ehmagawd, *five!*" she shouted.

"Yeah, we heard you." Lana rolled her eyes.

Massie sat back on her butt and placed a hand on her forehead. "That's it! Five pieces coming together!"

"Huh?" Shauna pushed her red glasses up her nose.

"I get it!" Massie leaned forward, dabbing her moist eyes with the top of her kneesock. "My charms are the five pieces. First we have to find them, *then* we'll come together."

"*Stawp*, I found two!" Lana dropped the diamond-encrusted bell and the horse into Massie's palm.

The horse was slightly scuffed, the bell unharmed. There was hope!

Massie scoured with renewed determination, her hands scraping over dust, spilled drinks, and discarded cocktail napkins. If it weren't for Hermia's promising prediction, she would have called off this degrading search mission before it even began. But those charms were no longer guilt-tokens from her absent parents. They were magical keys with the power to unlock her destiny. Totally worth a floor crawl.

"Can I keep the horse?" Lana asked, nibbling on her beauty mark. "You know, as a reward?"

"Yeah, and can I have the bell?" Shauna asked, squatting like a frog. "For helping?"

"What?" Massie snapped. *"No!"*

Shauna and Lana exchanged shoulder shrugs and stood.

Turning faster than yogurt in a hot car, they wiped their hands on their Burberry dresses and joined Ahnna and Brianna's condescending stare-circle.

"Who's ready for a live performance from Christina Aguilera?" Merri-Lee shouted from the stage.

"Eeeeeeeeeeee!" The Ahnnabes waved their hands, then rushed the stage with the rest of the guests, never once looking back to see if Massie was with them.

The pain of getting ditched like last year's Pucci print seized Massie's entire body. Her vision kaleidoscoped. Her limbs hung like an empty dress, her heart a squashed piece of bubble gum on the side of the road. Was she that easy to walk away from? That disposable?

Obviously.

The girls' Burberry plaid–clad bodies vanished into the dense crowd. And just like that, the Ahnnabees were gone, like a fading scene in a movie. A movie about a friendless girl desperate to find her missing charms or she would be forever doomed.

Spending hours in a dressing room while her swizzle stick–size sisters cursed carbs and saturated fats worked Dylan's appetite into a frenzy. Only this time, she didn't crave food. She craved *fun*.

"I'm going out to watch Christina," she announced to her sisters, who were still in the makeup chairs being preened like it was Fashion Week. It seemed criminal to watch the show on a dinky monitor when the performances were right there, just on the other side of the wall.

"Tell the girl she needs to eat," Jaime snarled at the TV. "That genie is gonna slip right out of her bottle."

"Hold still," urged Kali, clamping down on the eyelash curler. "I almost ripped your lashes off."

"Ohmigod, I would club a seal to look like Christina." Ryan dotted iridescent highlighter over her cheekbones. "She's got the whole hungry runaway look *down*."

"I'll let her know." Dylan rolled her eyes, then hurried out, finding it hard to believe they came from the same parents.

Backstage, the air was crackling with energy. On the dance floor it was blazing.

Dylan forced her way to the front of the crowd, just behind the mosh pit. Were people really moshing to "Come On Over"?

The whirlpool of spastic rain-dance moves looked like it would have been fun if it were a sneakers-and-sweats kind of day. But in YSL wedges, it was all about steering clear of harm and swaying gently with a less explosive bunch.

Dylan inched back a few feet and stood beside the four girls in ill-advised matching Burberry dresses. They were standing in a gossip cluster, threatening to destroy some girl they'd just fought with. Still, Dylan decided they were less dangerous than the pop pit.

Sexy servers weaved in and out of the crowd. Their recipe-covered catsuits added an edge to the party that was typical of her mother. Merri-Lee always did it better and bigger than anybody else. The packed house and fourteen-page waiting list proved it.

"Who's ready for a new year?" Christina called into the crowd.

Everyone cheered, especially Dylan, who had spent the last three hundred and sixty-four days playing it safe with the COCs (Children of Celebrities), her press-phobic friends, and was hungry for some action.

"Well, get ready for *this*!" Christina unzipped her satin jacket, revealing a black leather tube top, then swan-dived into the crowd. Fans passed her between them while the dancers kept the party going onstage. When Christina was ready to sing, the crowd lifted her stiff body back onto the stage as if loading a sarcophagus onto a truck. Now *this* was living!

Dylan's insides leapt like popping popcorn kernels. Why had she wasted so much time trapped in a stale dressing room with her sisters when she could have been out here, living *la vida loca*?

Then she remembered . . .

She didn't have anyone else. The COCs were away on family vacations. And living *la vida loca* solo was like riding a bicycle built for two—alone. What was the point?

Thwack!

A sharp object pegged Dylan's left ear. She looked up, suspecting a loose bead from the Yves. But the ceiling hadn't retracted yet, so any clutch-related fallout would have landed on the roof.

Thunk!

Owie! Dylan rubbed the right side of her neck. A crispy wonton lay lifeless by her shoe, dead like a bee after stinging. Either there was a disgruntled waitress in their midst or the universe was urging her to eat more.

Thwack!

Another wonton nailed her cheek. She eyed the Burberry girls, wondering if this had anything to do with their recent fight. But, engaged in a battle all their own, they continued close-talking, oblivious to the WMDs (wontons of mass destruction).

Dylan whipped around.

Thwack! Thwack! Thwack!

Three more WMDs hit her square in the face.

Ouch!

Two boys about her age, standing ten feet away, turned toward the stage and bit their bottom lips. Their shoulders shook with erupting laughter.

Flirting much?

Bending down while holding the snap on her pants closed just in case, Dylan scooped up the fallen WMDs. On her way up, more popcorn popped inside her. This had total fun potential!

The COCs would have dropped the wontons on the closest server's tray, wiped their hands of unwanted grease, and breathed a spearmint-scented sigh of disgust. But Dylan pulled back her arm, twisted her torso, and unleashed the apps like a softball pitcher on scout day. Two hit the shaggy blond and one pegged the brunette.

Ha! Not bad for a skinny girl!

They quickly searched the floor, hoping to fire back, but the wontons were squashed by a gaggle of Carrie Bradshaw wannabes teetering their way to the front of the crowd in last season's Manolos.

"Now what?" Dylan called, in love with her own bravado.

"Now we dump *these*"—the blond one held up a pack of Pop Rocks—"in the mango salsa." He wiggled his little butt like a happy puppy.

Dylan giggled. "What's your name?"

The boys exchanged a playful glance. They were both cute, but in different ways.

"I'm Dick Hurtz," snickered Shaggy.

"And I'm Dick Burns," grinned the pretty boy who, at closer look, had one green eye and one blue eye. He was definitely more movie star handsome than the other one. Still, Dylan was more drawn to Dick Hurtz, for his pranking genius.

"Nice to meet you," Dylan said to the Canine Chorus name tags pinned to their oxfords. Dick Hurtz was "Derrick." Dick Burns was "Cam." "My name is Harriett Weiner." She smirked. "But most people call me Harri."

They all cracked up together, completely unaware that Christina had finished her set and Merri-Lee was promising an introduction to her daughters after a few more songs from the DJ.

"Cool hair, Harri," Cam told her genuinely.

Dylan felt her red do, remembering that she was rolling with the half-curly half-straight, thanks to her needy sisters. "I didn't want to commit."

"Kinda like my eyes." Cam smiled.

Dylan smile-giggled.

"So, *Harri*, how'd you get into this party?" asked Derrick, dumping some Pop Rocks into his mouth. They crackled with delight, like his mischievous brown eyes.

Cam handed him a can of Coke. Derrick took a big sip. When his head didn't explode, they shrugged and turned their attention back to Dylan.

"Um, I came with some friends," she lied, fearing the pranks would stop if they knew she was related to the hostess. "What about you?"

"We're kind of working here." Cam smiled sweetly. "Our moms are volunteer trainers for the Canine Chorus. So we're kinda helping out."

"Doing *what*?" Dylan joked, as Derrick casually released a pinch of Pop Rocks into a passing woman's champagne flute. Veuve fizzed over the brim and trickled down her white-gloved arm. She screeched. They laughed.

"Pop Rockkkkkss!" Derrick burped.

"Dude." Cam blushed and then turned to Dylan. His blue and his green eye looked brighter. "He's not around girls very much. We go to Briarwood."

"OCD," Dylan groaned, as if admitting she went to an all-girls school would make him feel better.

"OC-DEEEEEEEEEEE," Derrick burped.

A Britney look-alike, dancing to Q-Tip's "Vivrant Thing," waved the air, then pulled her boyfriend away.

Dylan burst out laughing. "How d'you *do* that?"

"You actually wanna *know*?" Cam asked, shocked.

"Toe-dally." Dylan nodded, imagining herself burping words with the COCs. Maybe a little boy-humor was just what OCD needed to loosen up. Somehow, she doubted it.

"Stay here." Derrick pushed through the dense crowd like a running back, leaving Dylan and Cam on the packed dance floor. An exchange of friendly smiles and awkward glances around the party made it even more obvious that neither one of them had much experience with the opposite sex.

"I kinda wish we had boys at OCD," Dylan shouted over Q-Tip. "School would be more fun."

"Yeah." Cam stuffed his hands in his pockets, pulled out a handful of gummy sours, and opened his palm. "Want?"

"No thanks," Dylan politely declined. "I'm trying to lose weight." She waited a few seconds, hoping he'd take the bait.

"Why?" he mumbled.

Yes! Massie Blo— was wrong! Wrong and jealous!

"Yeah, you're right." Dylan shrugged. "Why?" She pinched a red sugarcoated bear and dropped it in her mouth. Cam ate a green one. They looked at each other and giggle-winced from the sour rush.

"Here!" Derrick appeared with two glasses of icy Coke. "Drink these super-fast."

Without question, Dylan did what she was told.

"As soon as that burp passes your throat, speak!" he explained. "Timing is everything. If you do it too soon, you'll puke."

Cam giggled, then popped another gummy in his mouth. He chew-winced and watched Dylan. Derrick was staring too. His butt wiggled slowly, like a tail starting to wag. He reminded her of a happy yellow Lab, and Dylan felt completely at ease . . . until her torso tightened with pressure.

"Something's happening!" She tapped her chest, encouraging the gas. Up it crept. Up . . . up . . . up . . . Slowly but steadily, the burp inched toward her throat. Stinging her ears and pushing past her tonsils, the invisible bubble reached its mark. Then, with grace and focus, Dylan bellowed . . .

"Co-ca Co-*laaaaaaaaaaaaaaaa!*"

The boys cracked up and high-fived her as if she had just scored the winning goal in some sport that had goals. Dylan's eyes watered, a little from the burp but mostly from the pride.

"I did it!"

"Wait until your friends hear you." Derrick beamed.

Dylan thought of the COCs and immediately knew that burping words would appeal to them about as much as a hidden camera in the girls' bathroom. Unless she could figure out a way to burp the who's who articles in the *Hollywood Reporter*, they probably wouldn't be interested. "I don't think they'd be that into it."

"Then you need new friends," Derrick insisted.

Dylan pressed her glossy lips together and nodded. He was right.

"'Scuse me," slurred a blond-bouffanted mom dressed in a tight black cocktail dress. A gold crown was on her head and an empty martini glass was dangling in her hand. "Would-ju mind taking our pik-chure?" She gestured to the other moms standing behind her, who were also wearing black dresses.

Dylan reached for the disposable camera. "Su—"

"I'll do it." Derrick grabbed it away with a devilish grin.

While the women linked arms and finger-fluffed their hair, Derrick aimed the camera down the back of his jeans and fired off three shots.

Dylan and Cam turned away, hiding their laughter.

"Harri, you are, like, the coolest girl we've ever met," Derrick told Dylan after he handed back the camera. "You're like a dude, but not."

Dylan's cheeks warmed from the compliment. "Thanks."

Cam nodded in agreement. "Do you play sports?"

"Nah." Dylan shook her head regretfully. "I'm too skinny."

Derrick nodded like he saw her point. "What's your real na—"

"Dylan!" Shouted a thin, Elmer's glue–colored man. "I've been looking everywhere for you." He pressed a finger against his headset and pushed a button on his walkie-talkie. "Got 'er. Have Merri-Lee's bodyguard meet us . . . dance floor . . . near the soda bar. . . . Over."

"Your real name is Dylan?" Derrick asked shyly. "I'm—"

"You're Derrick and he's Cam."

"How'd you know *that*?"

Dylan pointed at their Canine Chorus name tags and smiled smugly.

"Oh." He shrugged, a little embarrassed.

"Time to go," the stage manager said once Merri-Lee's hefty bodyguard arrived.

"Thanks for the lesson," Dylan whisper-giggled. "And the sours."

The boys both told her she was welcome, and smile-waved goodbye. It was obvious from the awestruck shimmer in their eyes that they thought she was special. A skinny, fun dude-chick with trendsetting hair, who'd burped a four-syllable name on her very first try.

Dylan sauntered away with the confidence of a Grammy-toting pop star. If they thought she was fun now, wait till they saw her on TV.

Kristen tossed her math book onto the coffee table. It landed with a thud, summing up her state of mind perfectly. Studying positive integers was the only "positive" in her entire night. And she couldn't even concentrate, because Ali had been yapping ever since she got baby Max back to sleep.

"What do you mean he was *flirting* with her?" Ali twirled her dirty-blond blowout. "Flirting like *talking*, or flirting like *touching*?"

Kristen rolled her eyes and turned on the TV. Merri-Lee Marvil's party was raging. The DJ was playing Lil' Bow Wow's "Bounce With Me" and judging by all the sweaty foreheads, it looked like the party guests had been bouncing with him for a while.

"You *have* to keep him away from her," Ali whispered into her cell phone, pacing in front of the TV. "I dunno, spill salsa on her lap, just do *something*!"

Mic in hand, Merri-Lee stepped into the foreground and began shouting over the music. "Make sure you stick around, because a very lucky girl is about to have her New Year's dreams come true when she gets kissed by ThRob over at our Orlando party."

They cut to a stunned blond girl with crooked bangs and round blue eyes standing in front of her house. She was dressed in a ridiculous red dress waving, metronome style, at the camera. Kristen hate-kicked her math book onto the floor. Even the freaks were having fun tonight!

"Tell him you're on the phone with me and that I say hi." Ali crossed in front of the TV. "Tell 'im. Tell 'im *now*. Go. Gogogogogo. Yeah, I'll wait!"

"Move!" Kristen waved Ali aside.

Ali responded by sticking out her tongue and middle finger.

Kristen turned up the TV.

"We're also going to see performances from . . ." Merri-Lee paused, and then looked down. She squinted in confusion while the rest of her forehead remained Botox-smooth. The camera pulled back to reveal a brunette, about Kristen's age, whispering something to Merri-Lee. Then she grabbed the mic from Merri-Lee's hand and addressed the crowd. Wearing kneesocks, wedges, and a black dress covered in metallic triangles, she had *Teen Vogue* style and *CosmoGirl* confidence.

"Excuse me, I have an announcement to make." Her alluring amber eyes were fixed on the uproarious guests, refusing to be discouraged by the chaos. Off to the side,

Merri-Lee was shaking her head and shrugging her bony shoulders, letting everyone know she had no clue who the girl was or what she was doing. But as always, Merri-Lee embraced spontaneity. Her end-of-year highlight shows were always hilarious because of it.

"I lost some very important charms," the girl shouted. "A dollar sign, a shoe, and a pig. If anyone finds them, please return them to me, Massie Block. My cell number is—"

Merri Lee grabbed the mic away from Massie. "Okay, that's enough. We don't want every creep on the planet calling you now, do we?" She giggle-petted Massie on the head.

"Watch the hair." Massie swept Merri-Lee's hand aside.

Kristen gasp-laughed. The girl had guts.

"Ha! What a hoot!" Merri-Lee took a step back to admire the intriguing stranger. "You sound like one of my daughters." Then she leaned in, as if confiding in Massie. "Wait, you don't think you're fat, do you?"

"Gawd, no." Massie put her hands on her hips and rolled back her shoulders. "I'm perfect." She winked into the lens.

Kristen burst out laughing. Was the girl joking or boasting? Not that it really mattered. She was exactly the kind of person Kristen needed in her life. Fearless. Flawless. Fabulous. *Fun!*

"Okay!" Ali shouted into her phone. "I promise I'll be there as soon as I possibly can. Yes, *alone*." She side-glared at Kristen. "It won't be too late—the Colemans are pretty dorky. They never stay out past—"

The front door clicked open.

"Gottagobye." Ali hung up her phone, slid her marshmallow-and-Coke concoction over toward Kristen, and then picked the math book off the floor. She plopped down on the couch and began leafing through the pages.

Kristen considered telling her that the book was upside down but didn't bother.

"Mr. and Mrs. Coleman!" Ali looked up. "What are you doing home so early? It isn't even midnight."

Mrs. Coleman gripped her mouth with one hand and her stomach with the other. Then she made a mad dash for the bathroom.

"Greta ate some bad sushi." Mr. Coleman loosened his tie. "She threw up five times at Merri-Lee's."

"You were at Merri-*Lee's*?" Kristen cried.

"Not the point," Ali said through clenched teeth. Then smiled with the compassion of a nun. "I pray she'll be okay. We should probably get going."

"There was bad sushi at Merri-Lee's?" Kristen wondered, unable to imagine anything being bad at that party.

"No, we ate before we got there." He pulled a money clip stuffed with bills out of his side pocket. "We stopped at my sister's house first. She took an international cooking class at the community center and made her own tuna hand rolls." He shuddered. "I warned her. I said, 'My sister can't make reservations. What makes you think she can cook?' But Greta insisted."

"Wow, that's too bad," Ali said, checking the time on the cable box. "I guess we better get going then."

"Listen," Mr. Coleman said, flipping through his cash, "I won't be able to take you home because, you know." He thumbed in the general direction of his barfing wife. "But I told our driver to drop you wherever you need to go."

"Awesome!" Ali stuffed the math book under her arm. "Hey Kristen, you may want to put your glass of whatever that is in the sink. It's rude to leave dishes."

"Oh, right. Sorry." Kristen stomped into the kitchen, vowing revenge on her cousin with every indignant step she took.

She returned to find Ali stuffing a wad of cash in her pocket.

"Thanks again, girls," Mr. Coleman said, ushering them toward the door. He tossed a gold dollar-sign charm on the front-foyer table, then extended his hand for a shake. "Happy New Year."

"Happy New Year to you, sir." Ali returned the gesture with Girl Scout gusto.

"What's that?" Kristen asked, eyeing the charm.

"Oh, just a little something Greta spotted on the ground at the party while she had her head between her knees. She wanted to take it home for good luck, but frankly, I don't think it's working."

Kristen picked it up and closed her fist around the gold charm.

"Would you like to have it?" Mr. Coleman asked before Kristen had the chance.

Too overwhelmed to speak, she nodded her head yes and was out the door before he could change his mind.

The limo smelled like cigar smoke and hair spray. "We're going back to Merri-Lee Marvil's party, please," Kristen told the driver, cracking the window.

He started the engine.

"No way!" Ali barked. "He's dropping me at Morgan's house." She pulled a pair of patent leather stilettos from her green-and-white L. L. Bean bag.

"Please," Kristen heard herself beg. Fate was calling. She had to answer. "I'll only be a minute. Then we can go wherever you want."

"*We?*" Ali snapped, hooking the stiff heel of her stiletto and forcing it over her heel.

"You're not going anywhere with me. You're going home." She leaned forward. "First stop, the Pinewood Apartments, and then we're going to 6783 Sycamore Crescent. Over by the high school."

"No, we're not." Kristen leaned forward too. "We're going to Merri-Lee's party, *then* Sycamore Crescent."

"Are not!" Ali unscrewed her mascara wand.

"Okay then." Kristen sat back on the black leather seats. "I'll just follow you to the party and tell everyone that sometimes you pick your nose and roll your boogers into a ball when you think no one is looking."

Ali punched the seat. Makeup scattered onto the floor. "You can't!" she pleaded.

"I can and I will." Kristen folded her arms across her red Juicy hoodie. "Unless we stop at Merri-Lee's first."

Ali checked the time on her cell phone. "You better be quick."

Kristen leaned back in her seat and closed her eyes.

It was finally time to enjoy the ride.

Alicia took the raucous applause for the Canine Chorus as a good sign. If people went this wild for three mutts who barked what sounded more like "Twinkle, Twinkle, Little Star" than like "Auld Lang Syne," surely they would go mad for BADSS. And if *they* didn't, *someone* would. Maybe a talent agent in L.A.? A pop star looking for a video honey? A Broadway director out to cast the next Maria in *West Side Story*? Millions of people were watching. At least a hundred of them could make Alicia's dreams come true.

Brooke and Alicia held hands in the wings, anxiously bobbing up and down on the balls of their Capezios.

"Forty-five seconds," said a male stage manager with bigger boobs than Alicia.

"Poor guy," Brooke mumbled, eyeing his chest.

"I know how he feels." Alicia glanced down at her bulging vest, where the glitter was starting to flake. She had deliberately worn a bra one size too small to be sure Thing One and Thing Two didn't try to jump out and steal the show.

"At least you *have* boobs." Poppy unbuttoned her vest to the belly button. "I'm so well proportioned it's boring."

Alicia and Brooke rolled their eyes but held their tongues. Poppy had learned the routine in fifteen minutes and saved their act. If it weren't for her well-proportioned body they'd still be listening to the mutts.

The houselights dimmed. Merri-Lee spoke into the mic.

"Up next we have some local talent. . . ."

This was it!

"Ahhhhhh." Alicia and Brooke squeezed each other's hands numb. Brooke squeezed because she was nervous. Alicia squeezed because she was on the verge of greatness. With Skye and her studio-owning, daughter-favoring parents two time zones away, Alicia would finally get the attention she deserved—and introduce Mrs. Fossier, and the world, to the *real* captain.

From the front row, Nadia Rivera flashed an encouraging thumbs-up to her daughter and dabbed her almond-shaped eyes with a handkerchief. Len put his arm around her and squeezed proudly. Alicia wanted to smile back at her parents with love, but all she could do was lift her hand in heartless acknowledgment. It was their fault her hairy calves were sweating in her leg warmers. And if that sweat was responsible for distracting her from her performance . . .

She blinked back the thought. Anything less than perfect was not an option.

"I am proud to introduce BADSS!" Merri-Lee gushed.

The audience applauded. The cameras turned to face them. Alicia's stomach dipped. Her ears rang. Her legs sparked with electricity. It was time for her mind to take five and let her body take over.

Shakira's "Ojos Así" blasted through the speakers, and the girls flick-kicked onto the stage. From there, they exploded with raw energy and refined talent. Poppy was punching every move in ways that And-rrhea never could. And the audience was going crazy. They whooped, clapped, and whistled. Cameras started flashing. The audience was dancing along. Alicia's mother began chanting her name and soon the entire party was chanting, "Alicia! Alicia! Alicia!" Their support and approval filled her with something lighter than air.

She danced with the grace of a swan and the strength of a bull. With every layout, twist, and triplet, Alicia grew confident—no, certain!—that her future as a captain-slash-superstar would be cemented in—

What the . . . ?

Her Capezio came down on what felt like a pebble; a slippery pebble that took her left foot for a skate while her right foot remained planted firmly in second position. Pulled in opposite directions, her legs felt like the rope in a ruthless game of tug-of-war. The next moment, Alicia was on her butt in a half split, struggling to breathe.

Brooke rushed to her side.

The camera lights dimmed.

The Shakira track stopped playing.

Merri-Lee decided to "check in" with the party in Orlando.

Alicia's ankle throbbed.

Her head spun.

Her heart was broken.

And Poppy had made off with her Marc Jacobs bag.

"You better be quick," Ali called from inside the limo.

"I will, I promise." Kristen slammed the door, exhaling a puff of air.

"Hurry!" Ali called one last time.

Kristen raced to the entrance, paying little mind to the shivering crowd of onlookers behind the gates, the giant purse at the top of a pole, or the red carpet—which was now littered with cigarette butts, silver gum wrappers, and empty water bottles. She was on a mission. And, as with everything she set her mind to, Kristen was determined to succeed.

Clutching the gold dollar-sign charm in her palm, she hurried past the snaking line of wannabe guests outside the door and marched straight to the front.

"Hi." She smiled brightly at the large gatekeeper in the white suit and matching fur hat. Cold wind blew against her sensitive Whitestripped teeth, sending a shock of pain that resonated all the way down to her frozen flip-flopped feet.

"Back o' the line!" shouted some grumpy man in a leather trench coat.

"Yeah!" shouted a woman in Lucite platforms and a tacky pink puffy coat. "Who do you think you are? One of those Olsen twins?"

"Where's your ticket?"

"You on the list?"

"Go home to Mommy!"

Others quickly joined in, cursing her out and wishing her harm for cutting the line.

Kristen finally turned to face her detractors. "I have *this*, okay?" She pinch-held the charm over her head, proving she had something more valuable than a ticket or a name on a list.

She turned back to the man in the white suit. "I'd like to get in now, please."

"So would they," he grumbled, chin-pointing at the angry mob behind her.

Kristen smiled politely. "I don't want to see the show, I just have to give something to my friend," she said, loving the way *friend* sounded.

"So do they." He chin-pointed again.

"No, but I really do. I'll just be a minute. Here . . ." Kristen searched her body for collateral. A watch, a tennis bracelet, diamond earrings. But she had nothing. Ironically, the only thing she had of value was the gold dollar sign. And she was there to give it back.

Tears began to fill Kristen's eyes. Tears she didn't even know she had. Yet there they were, in a state of permanent readiness. Destined to fall whenever she thought about things she couldn't afford—things that came so easily to everyone else.

"You just come from the gym?" the human marshmallow asked, like she would ever wear Juicy to the gym.

You just come from a marshmallow factory? she wanted to shout back. But a cluster of five hip hip-hoppers surrounded him and shut her out. The three guys were covered in Sean John logos and varying shades of Kangol hats. The two girls wore knee-high lace-up boots, their dresses covered by fur coats. While they gave their names to the Marshmallow, Red Kangol paced back and forth, talking on his cell and begging some girl in Queens to get her booty to Westchester.

"Take one of the label's choppers if you need to, baby. We're at the airport. The pilot can land right at the front door." He gestured toward the private planes parked in the distance, as if she could see them.

Kristen's eyes welled up again. She didn't even have a bike.

"Your name is on the list," Red Kangol insisted. He tilted his neck, gripped the cell with the side of his head, and rubbed his hands together for warmth. "It's so cold here without you, baby." He listened to her response while eyeing a gaggle of blondes in minidresses as they searched for the back of the line. "Nah, I understand. Happy New Year, Boo. I love you too."

He dropped his phone in the deep side pocket of his jeans.

"Lemme guess," Green Kangol mumbled. "Rihanna's not coming."

Marshmallow handed them their VIP stickers, then unhooked the red velvet stanchion. The five-pack sauntered inside, avoiding eye contact with the losers still stuck on line.

This set the mob off all over again.

"I've been standing here since Thanksgiving!"

"I can't feel my feet!"

"What makes *them* so special?"

"A recording contract!" Marshmallow shouted back.

Suddenly, Kristen sensed a billion tiny inchworms crawling up her arms. It was a familiar feeling—slightly ticklish, slightly irritating—one she got whenever she had a risky idea.

"Can I go in now?" Kristen smiled again. "My name is Rihanna."

Instead of checking the list, Marshmallow eyeballed her. It was that doubtful squint her overprotective mother had perfected years ago. Regardless of the situation, it always asked the same question: *Are you lying to me?*

"*What?* Why are you looking at me like that?" Kristen asked, feeling herself blush. "Check the list. You'll see. I'm there."

"Last name?" Marshmallow asked, haphazardly flipping through the pages on his clipboard.

Kristen's mouth dried. Her heart beat double time. The inchworms ran for their lives. *Now what?* She stood on her frostbitten but beautifully pedicured toes and peeked at his pages.

He pulled the clipboard back.

"Oh, come on," she pleaded. "I'm on there. Check *Rihanna*."

"No last name?"

"Ummm . . ."

Out of sheer desperation, Kristen released the dollar sign to the ground. It landed with a plink. "Oh no, my charm!" she gasped, before lightly stepping on it with her flip-flop. In a show of extreme panic she dropped to the frigid pavement. Through a veil of forced tears she whimpered, "Just check under *R*, okay?" She searched the ground in a frenzy of *don't mess with me* emotions.

Marshmallow, obviously too masculine to deal with a sobbing girl, flipped to the R's. "All right," he nose-sighed. "Here it is. Rihanna. No last name."

"Found it!" Kristen declared, holding up the charm.

Marshmallow handed her a VIP sticker with her new name on it and opened the door.

"Happy New Year, Rihanna," he grumbled.

"You too, M—" Kristen caught herself. "Mister." She hurried inside where it was warm.

Merri-Lee's *New Year's Yves* party looked different in real life than it did on TV. Less friendly. More chaotic. Completely overwhelming. Colored lights bounced from one hair-sprayed blowout to the next. Music pulsated. Tall people were everywhere. And no one was wearing Juicy.

Kristen hovered by the exit, shaking, like a terrified little flower girl about to walk the aisle at St. Patrick's Cathedral. What was she thinking? Was she really going in there alone? Where were the girls her age? Her legs stiffened. Her stomach locked. She panted nervously. Hovering next to the old people, who were hovering next to the circular bar, Kristen remained a safe distance from the raucous dance floor. How was she ever going to find Massie in this madhouse?

In an attempt to look like she belonged, Kristen helped herself to a grilled prawn off a passing waitress's tray. Pigs in a blanket would have made her happier, or maybe one of those mini microwavable egg rolls. But she was trying to look rich, and shrimp cocktail was always the most expensive appetizer on the menu.

And then, the four girls she'd seen on TV scurried by in their matching plaid dresses.

"'Scuse me?" Kristen called before she had any idea what to say.

They stopped. The one with the curly butterscotch blond bob was the first to turn.

"Yuss," she snarled.

"Ummm." Kristen took a step back, hating her mouth for writing a check her brain couldn't cash. "Uhhh . . ." She thought about coming right out and asking if they knew Massie but decided against it. They were probably famous. Better to see if they were friendly first. "How much longer until midnight?"

Curly hair checked the screen on her cell phone. "One hour and thirteen minutes." She took a step closer. "Don't worry"—she read the name on Kristen's VIP sticker— "*Rihanna*, that's plenty of time to change out of those sweats and into— *Stawp!*"

"*What?*" the other girls asked.

"Did you see her name?" Curly waved her hands like a baby chick trying to fly.

The girls leaned into Kristen's chest.

"Her name is Reee-*ahnna*!" Curly announced. "She's an Ahnna!"

"Eeeeeeeeeeeeee!" They all began shaking their hands and hopping around.

"I'm Ahnna." Curly opened her arms and pulled Kristen in for a sweaty hug. She smelled a little like French onion dip.

"Stawp!" Red Glasses extended her hand. "I'm Shauna."

"Lana." A girl with a beauty mark above her lip smile-waved.

"Brianna," said the one with black bangs.

Three babysitter-age girls dressed like college girls giggled as they walked by.

"Are you a new girl group?" Kristen asked, wishing she had a pen for autographs.

"Pretty much." Shauna beamed.

"We're the Ahnnabees," Lana said proudly.

"Because all of our names have Ahnnas in them," Brianna explained.

"You know . . ." Ahnna hooked her arm through Kristen's. "We're looking for a new member," she whispered. "We lost one tonight."

"Oh." Kristen tried to sound sympathetic while quickly scanning the crowd for Massie Block. "Sorry for your loss."

"Hakuna matata." Ahnna made a peace sign. "She wasn't a true Ahnna. Not like you."

"Huh?" Kristen tuned back in to the conversation. "But I can't sing. I'm more into soccer and stuff."

"You don't have to *sing*." Ahnna giggled. "You just have to be an Ahnna and you, Reee-*ahnna*, are a true Ahnna."

"Oh." Kristen looked down at her name tag. "This is not—"

"Give her the quiz!" Brianna interrupted, bouncing up and down.

"Yeah, the quiz!" Lana echoed.

"Can I ask the first question?" Shauna pushed her red glasses up the bridge of her nose.

"What quiz?" Kristen asked with growing interest.

"It's mostly about your favorite things," Ahnna explained. "You know, to see if we have anything in common other than our names." She winked. "Even though I can tell by that VIP sticker that we already do."

"The thing is . . ." Kristen giggled, suddenly excited to share her secret. Excited to laugh about the clever way she swindled Marshmallow. Excited that Ali was stuck waiting for her in the car. "I kind of snuck in here tonight."

Their eyes widened, encouraging her to continue.

"My real name is Kristen," she blurted. "I came to find some girl named Massie. She lost this charm and—"

"Security!" shouted Ahnna.

"What?" Kristen gasped.

"Secur-i-teeeeeee!" she shouted again.

Instead of waiting to find out what had gone wrong, Kristen bolted for the door marked VIP. She burst inside and crashed head-on into a thick white wall.

"Ahhhhhhhhhhh!" shouted the wall.

Kristen looked up. It was Marshmallow. And he was covered in burning hot coffee.

"What are you doing back here?" she asked, taking a step back.

"I'm on my break." He scowled and then grabbed her by the hood of her sweatshirt.

"Where are we going?" Kristen trembled.

"*You're* going outside."

"But I thought you were on break." She smiled, laying on the charm.

"Break's over!" Marshmallow chucked his empty coffee cup in the trash, dragging Kristen and her charm toward the nearest exit.

Everyone envy-stared as Merri-Lee's bodyguard led the Marvil girls to the stage. No one knew who they were *exactly*, but it was obvious from their matching outfits, flawless makeup, and three-hundred-pound escort that they were special.

Digital cameras flashed in their faces, each spark of light charging Dylan's mood. She waved at the guests, blew kisses to the cute ones, and smiled widely for lenses of all sizes. Could Derrick and Cam see her?

Jaime and Ryan, however, lifted their chins, rolled back their shoulders, and scowled. They were obviously trying to project "bored supermodel" but gave off "constipated cadet" instead.

The bodyguard cleared a path with his giant chest and placed the girls at the foot of the stage.

"Um, sir . . ." Ryan cupped her updo. "We're supposed to be *awn* the stage, not under it."

The bodyguard grunted and shook his head no.

"Whaddaya mean, *no*!?" We're Merri-Lee's *daughters*!" Jaime shouted loud enough for everyone to hear.

A cluster of over-hair-sprayed moms inched closer and began taking their pictures. Dylan threw her arms around her sisters and smiled brightly while Jaime and Ryan continued arguing.

"He's right," interjected a stage manager. "You girls will be down here. Your mom wanted it to seem like you were having fun at the party. The camera will find you, don't worry."

"Paaaaarty!" Dylan threw her hands in the air, snap-swaying to the Smash Mouth remix the house DJ began playing after Christina's short set. Smash was hardly her favorite, but it was better than listening to her sisters complain.

Not that she had a choice. Ryan and Jaime were all she had. Most of the girls at school were only interested in Dylan's famous mom, so she stuck close to her sisters, who were only interested in themselves.

A man dressed in black appeared with a big TV camera. He flicked on a blinding light, then began swaying back and forth; in her face . . . away from her face . . . in her face . . . away from her face. . . . How many millions of people were seeing this?

Drinking up the light like a sunflower, Dylan danced harder. Arms waving overhead, black cashmere tank sliding up her belly, leather-encased booty undulating, exfoliated feet balancing in gold wedges, hair half-straight half-curly smacking the side of her face. . . . The more her sisters argued with the bodyguard, the more solo airtime she was getting. It was perf—

Whaah??

Dylan's gold YSL stomped down on something fleshy. *Sashimi?*

"My *hand*!" shouted a girl from the floor.

"Stop the camera!" Dylan held her palm in front of the camera.

"I wasn't rolling," the cameraman said. "Just testing light."

"Oh." Dylan pouted, wishing she hadn't busted out her A-game for his lens.

"Offa my *hand*!" shouted the girl again.

"Oops, sorry." Dylan lifted her foot, then quickly crouched to assess the damage.

Pop! Her belly tsunamied from her pants. *What is up with this button???*

"Are you okay?" she asked, lowering her upward-creeping cashmere tank.

"No!" The girl's amber eyes were moist.

It was her! Massie Blo—.

"What're ya doing down there?" Dylan stood. "Looking for friends?"

"You're the one who should be looking for friends." Massie stood too; their eyes locked.

"What's *that* supposed to mean?" Dylan's cheeks warmed.

"You're still wearing those pants." She half smiled. "A real friend wouldn't let you do that."

"What is so bad about these pants?" Dylan stomped her foot.

"Look." Massie pointed at the "last-minute mirror" propped by the side of the stage for artists to have one last look before performing.

Dylan stomped over.

"Where are you going?" called the bodyguard.

But Dylan ignored him and approached the mirror with gusto, anxious to prove what she already knew. Dylan Marvil was thin. Possibly too thin. And her pants were just poorly made.

Dylan eyed her reflection.

Ahhhhhhhh! Fat-a-touille!

This mirror made her thighs bulb, her abs pooch, and her cheeks chipmunk. Her only slim feature was the left side of her hair, the part Kali had straightened.

"See?" Massie half smiled again.

Did she have to be so perfect looking aaaand so right?

Dylan swallowed the double cheeseburger–size lump in her throat. There had to be a logical explanation. Had to be . . . had to be . . . had to . . . and then she found it. And just like that, her angst melted like a bite-size Butterfinger in her back pocket.

"The only thing I *see*," she managed, "is one of those TV mirrors."

"What's a *TV mirror*?"

Dylan rolled her eyes, as if a lifetime of explaining "the biz" to average Janes was exhausting.

"It adds ten pounds to people so they know what they're gonna look like on TV."

Massie pushed Dylan aside. "Funny," she said to her reflection. "I still look thin."

Confusion bubbled inside Dylan like a shaken Pepsi. What was going on? Who was this girl and why was she so intent on destroying Dylan's confidence? Was she jealous? Evil? Or . . . *right*?

Impossible! She had to be jealous. Everyone else was.

"Let's go!" The stage manager tugged Dylan's arm and dragged her back to the stage.

Ryan and Jaime were trying to convince some dad in a leather suit to hold their lip glosses until their segment was over. "We don't want the home audience to see them in our pockets and think they're bulges of faaaat," Ryan explained.

"'Course not." The guy took the tubes and stuffed them in the inside pocket of his jacket, next to the cigars. Seconds later he was off, chasing his angry girl-friend.

"Is he trying to *steal* those?" Jaime tugged her ironed hair.

"Focus!" The stage manager clapped once. The girls finally gave him their attention.

"Now remember, your mother is going to talk about the little Christmas trip you took downtown to feed the homeless. The camera will cut to you girls in the audi-ence looking all happy and charitable, and then it will show the video." He chuckled as if remembering a funny joke. "Dylan, there's a great moment where you're hid-ing behind your mom, chowing an Entenmann's doughnut that is obviously supposed to be for one of the homeless people." He laughed again. "It's classic!"

Dylan covered her mouth in shame. What if Massie and the TV mirror were right? What if she *was* fat? She *had* eaten a lot of doughnuts that night. And the night after that . . . and the night after that . . . and—"Oh, no!"

"Don't worry," the man assured her. "It's exactly what this emotional piece needed. A little comic relief. The audience is gonna *love* it."

Dylan smiled uneasily, hoping he was right.

Merri-Lee took the stage and introduced her "girlies" to the world. Ryan and Jaime didn't even show teeth when their names were called. They simply glared at their mother, silently cursing her for not putting them onstage. Dylan, wanting to come off as the fun one, beamed when Merri-Lee introduced her. Then she blew kisses to fans and smooched the lens of the camera, leaving behind a perfect strawberry-scented smear. The audience cheered until she waved them off in an *I don't deserve your love* sort of way and lowered her eyes in mock shyness.

And then, out of nowhere, she had one of those moments. The kind your memory holds on to like a snapshot.

A gold object winked at Dylan from the concrete floor, its glare so strong it usurped the camera's bright lights, making her forget she was on TV. Without hesitation, she leaned down to pick it up. And then . . .

. . . *rrrrriiiippppppp*.

A group of girls behind her burst out laughing. The back of her pants split. *Did Cam and Derrick see?* Fortunately the house lights dimmed so they could roll the Christmas video. But there was just enough light for Dylan to see the object in her palm. It was a gold pig charm.

And it seemed to be oinking at her.

Zadrienne stopped his red Prius under the carport of the Victorian-style hotel. Parking attendants dressed in peach-colored capri pants and puffy-shouldered blouses directed sunburned guests to the New Year's Eve party in their ballroom. Groups of teens, swinging purses and ponytails, jammed into the revolving doors with giddy excitement. And music thumped from the various beach parties, guaranteeing a good time to anyone who could get in. If Sari and Mandy hadn't been sitting on her dress, Claire wouldn't have been able to contain her excitement.

A chipper blue-eyed attendant poked his head in the window. "Which party are you here for?"

"Batman's!" Todd called from the hatch in the back. He was lying in fetal position, jammed between Zadrienne's stinky baseball uniform and dozens of empty Gatorade bottles.

"Ignore him," Zadrienne huffed. "We're here to see—"

"ThRob!" the girls shouted from the backseat.

Zadrienne half turned. "Chill, okay!" he snapped. "I'll

do the talking." He turned back to the attendant. "One of these freaks won a contest."

"Me!" Claire called. "I won Dr. Party's radio contest!"

"Whooooooooo!" the girls shouted.

"Congratulations," smiled the guy, revealing a row of overbleached teeth. "Name?"

"Claire Lyons," she announced proudly, wondering if maybe he had heard her on the radio.

The attendant pressed a foamy headphone into his ear and spoke. "Glenn for Stacey. Come in, Stacey. I have a girl here who claims . . ." He turned his back to the Prius and continued.

"Can you believe ThRob are inside???" Sari tapped her ruby red slippers.

"Eeeeeeeeeeeeeeee!" The girls shook their heads and stomped their feet.

"Quitit!" Zadrienne hollered.

"Zay, stop screaming!" Kelsey barked. Her face flamed red.

The attendant poked his head back in the window. "You've been cleared." He smiled. "Now, what you're gonna wanna do is head to the very back of lot G and look for the big gray tour bus. You can't miss it. It has a beautiful airbrushed scene of wild horses painted on the side. The boys are in there."

"Aren't they in the hotel?" Mandy asked. "At the party?"

"Or the beach?" Sarah practically whined.

The attendant poked his entire face in the car. "Gosh no," he whispered. "They're terrified of crowds. Their broadcast will be coming from the tour bus."

The girls exchanged a puzzled glance, allowing their brains time to process the new information.

"Eeeeeeeeeeeeee!" they squealed again.

"We'll get to see where they sleep!" Claire shouted.

"And eat!" Mandy added.

"And watch TV!" Sarah chirped.

"And snack!" Sari tried.

"And poop!" Todd called from the back.

"Kill me," Zadrienne mumbled as he pulled away.

"Maybe I will." Kelsey leaned her head against the window and sighed.

After a brief moment of silence, Sari shouted "Again!"

On cue, the girls began giggle-singing ThRob's hit, "Twice the Fun," for the seventh time.

Baby, don't say we're done,
We know you are the one,
The rays to our sun,
We're begging you not to run,
Loving both of us is twice the fun.

Our parents taught us how to share,
They showed us how to care,
They gave us soft thick hair,
And a ton of fashion flair,
You know you like to stare.

We're begging you not to run,
Loving both of us is twice the fun.

When you're dating twins,
Everybody wins,
It's not a cardinal sin,
To get back twice what you put in.
Do you hear the violins?

Do you hear the violins?
Do you hear the violins?
Do you hear the violins?

We're begging you not to run,
Loving both of us is twice the fun.

"Get out of my car!" Zadrienne yelled, pulling up beside the tour bus.

The girls bolted like the seats were on fire.

"Let me out!" called Todd from the hatch.

Claire ignored him. She loved her brother but certainly didn't need him around for her first kiss.

The girls rapped on the bus doors with one hand and smoothed their hair with the other until the doors accordioned open.

"Name?" asked a husky man with a triangular black beard that practically touched his cleavage.

"Claire Lyons." She smiled, catching a whiff of burnt microwave popcorn. "I won Dr. Party's contest on the radio. The guy at the hotel told me to come here."

Even though he was wearing mirrored Oakleys, Claire sensed he was eyeing her Civil War–era dress.

"I'm T-Rex," he grumbled. "The boys' manager."

"Hi, T-Rex," the girls trilled as if greeting a birthday party clown.

"Come in." He stepped back, making room.

The girls piled on, but T-Rex stopped them with his meaty palm. "Just Karen."

"Claire," she corrected shyly.

"What about *us*?" Sari whined to her ruby red slippers.

"No go, Dorothy," T-Rex insisted. "The bus is too small. The boys are claustrophobic. You're shedding glitter. And you look like something right off Bourbon Street at Mardi Gras. Wait outside."

"For an *hour*?" Mandy smacked her princess skirt.

Claire wanted to protest but didn't have a chance. T-Rex shut the doors and ordered Claire to wait on the black leather couch. Then he slipped behind a blue curtain, leaving her alone surrounded by nothing but mirrors. No junk food, no bras from groupies, no video games or crumpled-up napkins with song lyrics. Just the reflection of a girl in a flashy red dress, navy blue Keds, and green hair glitter, waiting for her first kiss.

M'gosh! My first kiss!!!!

Claire's mouth went dry. Her heart clomped like a Clydesdale. Her cuticles begged to be picked. She was about to get kissed. By a pop star. On television. In front of the world!

Eyes open or closed? Head-tilt left or right? Tongue or no tongue? *Oh gosh, please, no tongue!* She had no idea what to do. All she knew was that this kiss had to be perfect. Not so much for her public image, but for her private one. The public would forget all about it as soon as they turned off their TVs, but Claire would remember it forever.

"I refuse to touch another contest winner," shouted a boy inside ThRob's tour bus. "The last one's lips were so chapped I practically bled. And the one before that smelled like salmon."

Claire quickly applied a waxy coat of cherry Chap-Stick.

"He's right," added a different boy. "It's not sanitary."

"I don't care if she has a mustache and a rotten tooth that spits fire," shouted T-Rex. "One of you is giving her a kiss at midnight. It's in the contract."

"She has a mustache?" asked the first boy.

The boys cracked up.

Claire's stomach lurched. She turned to the mirror and examined her top lip. It looked hairless, at least in this light. But still. How could she allow her first kiss to come from someone who didn't want anything to do with her? Sure, she was a fan, but she also had pride. Besides, the whole idea was to spend New Year's Eve with her best friends. And they were stuck in a parking lot wearing random costumes with her babysitter and little brother.

"Hey, maybe we should use that breath spray that smells like puke," the second boy suggested. "That would scare her off."

"Good idea," said one of the twins.

Claire jumped to her feet and hurried toward the door, totally freaked out. But then, the walls of the tour bus fell to the ground. A barrage of lights flooded the parking lot and throngs of screaming girls raced out from behind the cars. Behind her, Merri-Lee Marvil's face appeared on a gigantic drive-in movie–size screen.

"T-Rex, introduce her to the boys!" she gushed from her party in Westchester.

The manager tore down the blue curtain, lifted Claire into his King Kong arms, and placed her down between Theo and Rob. Shirtless and buff, one had a giant tattoo of the letter T across his chest and the other had an R. Claire felt like she was watching herself from someone else's body.

They greeted her with smiling chocolate brown eyes that appeared orange under the lights. Their thick black eyelashes and deeply tanned skin were even more pronounced in real life than they were in magazines and videos. Claire felt like the white center between two dark wafers of an Oreo cookie.

"You've been ThRobbed!" Theo pulled her in for a squeeze. He didn't smell like puke at all. More like Red Bull and pine-scented deodorant.

"We had hidden cameras behind the mirrors," Rob explained with a devilish smile.

"It was a prank!" Theo called.

The audience cheered while Claire replayed the last ten minutes in her head . . . loading on the ChapStick . . . checking her mustache in the mirror . . . trying to escape. . . .

"Don't worry," he added. "You don't have facial hair."

Claire covered her mouth shyly.

"Yes, she does!" shouted a boy in the front row. It was Todd, sitting on Zadrienne's shoulders, drumming his strawberry blond head. Mandy, Sari, and Sarah were waving wildly. Kelsey was picking at her green nail polish.

Claire's teeth began chattering. She had never been more excited in her entire life.

"This is for you." Rob handed Claire a red ring box. "For being such a good sport."

"Thanks." She dropped the box in her dress pocket. Her hands were way too shaky to open it in public.

"Wasn't she great, Merri-Lee?" Rob turned and asked the screen.

"Oh, she was," gushed the hostess via satellite. "But the real gift will come at midnight when Theo and Rob sing 'Twice the Fun' to our lucky winner and finish it off with a kiss," she reported. "Don't go away. Merri-Lee's *New Year's Yves* will continue with a lot more surprises, after the break."

The screen went blank and the camera lights shut off. Dancing white spots marred Claire's vision. Or was it her proximity to the two cutest boys in the four-oh-seven?

Theo took a step back and admired Claire. "Rad dress."

"Really?" Claire grinned, aware of the envious eyes staring up at her from the audience.

"Totally." Rob winked. "You're a real cutie."

"Thanks." Claire giggled, tipsy with love. They were totally first kiss–worthy. And apparently, so was she.

"There she is!" a familiar woman's voice shouted. Claire's body, sensing danger, shot a rush of adrenaline to her heart, filling her with a sickening sense of dread.

The cameras turned back on.

"What's happening?" asked Theo as two security guards and a woman dressed in a pea-green empire-cut dress hurried toward Claire.

"Mom?"

"Wait." Rob smiled. "Is this a payback prank?"

"I wish," Claire mumbled as her father elbowed his way to the front of the crowd, pulled Todd off Zadrienne's shoulders, and fired Kelsey on the spot.

"Looks like you're gonna have to kiss something else at midnight," Judi Lyons snapped at Rob. "Perverts," she muttered, yanking her daughter away.

"Mom!" Claire gasped, too mortified to look back at ThRob. "Don't do this to me!"

"What I did to you?" Judi's silver teardrop earrings bashed against her clenched jaw. "Imagine how I felt? Standing at a party and seeing my daughter on TV, dressed like Scarlett O'Hara, announcing to the world that she will be ravaged by twin hooligans at midnight?"

"No one was going to *ravage* me," Claire pleaded as

her mother, with the help of two security guards, pulled her away from the scene. But pleading was useless.

Everything was useless. She had never seen her mother so angry.

The ride home was silent, except for the occasional sniffle from Sari, who was certain she'd be sent to military school. And a quick exchange between her parents about someplace called Westchester.

Wherever that was . . .

The line outside Hermia's tent was still Harry Potter–long. And judging by the lack of wedding rings, most of those women wanted the psychic to promise them princes. But not Massie. She wanted to be queen.

Like last time, she raced to the front of the line with urgency, as if carrying a life-or-death message for Hermia—which she kind of was. Only the "life" part of the message had to do with Massie's social life. And the "death" part referred to its current state. She was officially friendless on the biggest night of the year, and would stay that way unless Hermia told her exactly what she needed to do to become a true leader. And this time, she refused to take "figure it out yourself" for an answer.

"Where do you think you're going?" slurred a woman wrapped in a baby blue pashmina.

"It's not decent to cut!" called some mom who obviously mistook Massie for someone who cared.

A few other comments whizzed by like music from a

passing car. But Massie tuned them out. *Mylifeisruined-MylifeisruinedMylifeisruined* was all she heard.

"I have no friends, thanks to you!" she shouted, storming into the Moroccan pillow–filled tent. "You're a real psychic like Dr. Dre is a real MD."

Hermia opened her gold-dusted lids as if woken from a nap. "You again?" She released her client's hand.

The chai smell had been overpowered by a nauseating mix of holiday perfumes.

"Do you need a minute with your daughter?" asked a familiar-looking woman, blowing into a tissue.

"My *daughter*?" scoffed Hermia.

"Oh, I remember you," Massie blurted, taking in the woman's red nose and lap full of crumpled pink Puffs tissues. "You're the one who likes Rick."

"*Liked!*" she quickly corrected. "After you told me he was here, I went out to find him and he was *gone*. He couldn't wait five minutes for me."

Massie paced across the dusty Oriental rugs, shaking her head as if horrified by the nerve of it all.

"I told you." Hermia sat back on her stack of pillows and ran a hand through her vibrant red hair. "Rick is still with his wife. And he is staying with her. You need to move on."

"I know." Jenna blew into a pink Puffs. "I know."

"Are you really gonna listen to her?" Massie snapped,

remembering her own crisis. "Thanks to her 'advice,' I have no friends, no bracelet, and no hope." She slammed the purple stone on the scarf-wrapped table. "Take it. It doesn't work."

"I meant what I said," Hermia insisted. "The five pieces will be joined at midnight." She checked her cell phone. "And it's almost midnight. So you better go."

"Where am I supposed to *go*?" Massie's throat locked.

"Didn't you hear?" Hermia asked with a Cheshire cat grin. "A young dancer slipped on a charm during her performance. She's backstage right now getting iced."

"What?"

The psychic stood, shuffled over to Massie, and pulled her into a hug. "Hermia is never wrong," she whispered, her breath smelling like Halls Mentho-Lyptus. "Now go," she urged. "Go!"

Massie hurried out of the tent, not quite sure if Hermia actually knew something or was just trying to get rid of her. Still, with the help of a fifty-dollar bribe, she bulldozed her way backstage just in case. A small object was knocking against the outside of her thigh while she walked. Without stopping, she dug her hand inside her dress pocket and gasped. The purple stone was back.

But how? Who? *When?*

Massie began to run, fueled by questions she couldn't answer. A mystery she couldn't solve. A destiny she couldn't reach. And the hope that with every frenzied step, she was getting closer.

Pushing past the backstage riffraff, Dylan stomped toward her mother's dressing room. Eminem's "The Real Slim Shady" blared from behind its closed door. Her temper was hot but her backside was cool, thanks to the six-inch split in the rear of her pants.

"Yazzzzz-min!" She burst through the door, gold YSL wedges blazing. It smelled like salsa and fruit-scented products. "Your Guccis are for hoochies!" She whipped her leopard faux-fur collar on the floor.

"What?" Yasmine turned down the music. Humid fog clouds swirled around the stylist as she steamed the rejected clothes that had been kicked, clumped, and tossed by the Marvil sisters.

"My pants ripped on the air!" Dylan turned around and wiggled her exposed butt as proof. "Where'dja get them? EBay?"

Kali, who was in the midst of pulling red hair chunks from her brushes, turned away, obviously not wanting to get involved. But it was too late for that. The whole *world* was involved.

"I just flashed ham on a global broadcast, thanks to these terrible pants you made me wear," Dylan shouted, her heart pounding. "What happened? Did you buy a pair of Bebes and slap a Gucci tag on the back, then charge my mom for—"

"Enough!" Yasmine barked, her bottom teeth jutting out like a bulldog's. With cheeks flushed from the hot steam, she clomped over in her angry black boots and grabbed Dylan by the wrist.

"Owie," Dylan moaned.

But Yasmine only tightened her grip.

"Maybe you beefed up a little over the holidays." She dropped Dylan's arm and took a step back, as if expecting to be slapped.

"*Please!* I wish." Dylan scoffed. "All I do is eat. And every time I look in the mirror I see skin and bones. I'm starting to think I have a tapeworm."

Yasmine rolled her eyes, then bit her thumbnail.

"Wait a minute." Clarity snapped the back of her neck like a hair elastic. Dylan inched toward Yasmine's dewy face and squinted suspiciously. "I know what you're doing." She nodded slowly, like a smug detective who just cracked a case. "You're trying to put this on me."

"That's *it*!" Yasmine huffed, meeting Dylan's green eyes with her hazel ones, then exhaling the smell of corn chips.

Kali turned up the music.

"You want to know what's happening here?"

Dylan raised her eyebrows and nodded yes in an *oh, this is gonna be good* sort of way.

Yasmine glanced at Kali. Kali shrugged as if to say, *Go for it. It's your life.*

"Fine. I'll tell you." Yasmine exhaled. "I got sick of your mother and sisters complaining that they were fat so I brought in skinny mirrors. They shave ten pounds off when hung straight, fifteen when tilted."

Dylan considered this for a moment. She could see how the stylist would be driven to such lengths. After all, her sisters were thin-sane. But that didn't explain the other mirrors in her life.

"What about the ones at home?"

"I had them replaced with skinny mirrors when you were in Saint Martin over Christmas." Yasmine leaned against her sewing table and folded her arms across her flat chest.

"What about our hotels?" Dylan tried.

"Replaced."

Dylan's insides sank. Or was that feeling her fat cells creating more space for their friends?

"What about the dressing rooms at the mall?"

"Oh, those are just tilted," Yasmine explained.

Dylan exhaled months of denial. A slab of skin curled

over the top of her pants like a pouting lip. Had it always been there? Images from the last year of her life sped through her mind like a TV show rewinding.

A bag of cheese-flavored Combos . . . two slices of ham and pineapple pizza . . . chips and salsa . . . chips and guac . . . chips . . . caramel latte with whip . . . extra whip . . . two brownies . . . chicken BLT . . . extra B . . . extra mayo . . . waffles and sausage . . . mixed berries . . . crème fraîche . . . hot chocolate . . .

And that was just today.

The sting that comes with realizing you've been lied to prickled and itched Dylan's skin. Her mouth dried. Her lashes fluttered. She was having another snapshot moment. It could be titled "the moment Dylan lost her innocence." Or "the moment Dylan stopped trusting people." Or "the moment Dylan became fat."

She smacked the pants that had betrayed her. The leather felt cold and unapologetic. "Size four?" She tugged at the label. "Did you fake that too?"

Yasmine looked away guiltily.

"Oh my Gawd, you did!" Dylan stomped her gold wedge. "I am so suing you!"

"Dylan, wait!"

"No, *you* wait!" Dylan shouted, not quite sure exactly what she meant.

And with that, she stormed toward the door and

marched out. It didn't matter that there was a huge tear in the back of her pants. Or that her blue-and-green polka-dot underwear was showing.

She had already been exposed.

If there was a feeling more pathetic than being the last kid in the school parking lot, waiting for Mom to arrive, Kristen was feeling it now. Seated backstage on a cracked plastic chair by the VIP entrance, she was crying into the terry-cloth sleeve of her sweatshirt, wishing harm on the happy performers who slowed down to stare when they entered. Hoping Marshmallow would stop staring at her. Praying her cab would arrive before tears shrank her Juicy.

Being kicked out of the party by Marshmallow for "impersonating Rihanna" had been a particularly low moment. Leaving without returning the dollar-sign charm had been rock bottom. And watching Ali pull away in the limo had been subterranean. But when her mom found out she'd spent her emergency money on a cab from the airport hanger party she'd crashed, and ridden alone, Kristen would be buried alive.

"Here." Marshmallow finally handed her a crumpled-up napkin from his inside pocket. It smelled like coffee. "Everything is going to be fine."

Then why are you hovering over me like a prison guard?
Kristen wanted to shout. Instead, she took the napkin
and wiped the corners of her eyes. He had been standing watch over her for the last forty minutes. His dark
brown eyes filled with a mix of disappointment and pity.
It was nothing she didn't already feel.

Just then, the pretty redheaded girl from her school
burst through the door. As usual, she was dressed like a
runway model. Her face was also streaked with tears.

Kristen looked up and tried to smile, silently acknowl-
edging that they were both crying on New Year's Eve.

"Ugh!" the girl sobbed. "There are people *everywhere*!"

"Everything okay, Ms. Marvil?" asked Marshmallow.
The burly bouncer looked confused, almost afraid, to be
surrounded by sobbing tweens.

She sniffle-nodded yes, then casually placed her hands
over her butt and began backing up toward the wall, as
if covering up an embarrassing stain.

"Are you related to Merri-Lee Marvil?" Kristen asked,
forgetting herself for a second.

"Yeah. I'm Dylan. Don't you go to OCD?" she asked,
sounding more suspicious than interested.

Kristen nodded. "I play soccer," she said, hoping that
might explain why they hardly knew each other.

"What are you doing here?" Dylan asked, hand-drying
her cheeks.

"I—" Kristen peered up at Marshmallow, silently asking if he would let her fib. He shrugged like he was too exhausted to care. "I was already inside but some spaz waiter spilled cocktail sauce all over my Chanel dress and I had to run out and change. Thank Gawd I had a pair of Juicy sweats in the limo. I'm Kristen." She smiled, realizing she hadn't really answered the question.

"Why are *you* crying?" Dylan eyed the red velour pants with interest.

"My cousin took off with the limo. I'm stuck waiting for a cab."

Marshmallow looked away, shaking his head in disbelief.

"Why didn't you leave with her?"

What was with all the questions?

"Oh, um, because I found this charm on my way out. I heard some girl lost it and I wanted to return it." Kristen swallowed hard, her heart pounding against the inside of her chest as if trying to tip Dylan off to her many lies.

"No way!" Dylan jammed her hand inside her tight leather pocket. "I found a charm too."

"What is it?" Kristen leaned forward, teeth chattering.

Dylan held her hand out dismissively.

"Oh, a pig." Kristen smiled. "Cute."

Dylan quickly stuffed the charm back in her pocket.

Then, as if contemplating something important, her emerald green eyes wandered. She twirled one of her long red curls. When she let go, it bounced back into place. "Where do you live?"

"Um, the Montador Building," Kristen lied again. But her building, the Pinewood Apartments, was next door to the luxury condos, so it wasn't too bad. "Why?"

"I'll make you a deal," Dylan offered, her eyes sharply focused on Kristen. "Trade outfits with me and I'll give you a ride home after the show."

"Yeah, right." Kristen giggled, assuming the proposition was a joke. The *G*'s stamped into the leather either stood for Gucci or Gap. Either way, they were nicer than anything she'd ever owned.

"I'm *serious*." Dylan pressed her butt against the door.

"Shoes too?"

"Everything." Dylan began unbuckling her wedges.

"I'm more of a silver person," Kristen added, trying to sound like she was settling. "But okay."

"Come on. Let's go change." Dylan pulled her by the hand. Marshmallow stepped aside, unwilling to argue with the boss's daughter.

"Cancel the cab," he said into the curly wire clipped to the white lapel of his suit. "Have fun." He smiled as Kristen reentered the world of the rich and famous.

"We will." She smiled back.

Now that she wasn't alone, the crowded dance floor looked like a dimly lit dream about supermodels in a club made of gold. It smelled like Kobe beef and exotic perfume. It felt more luxurious than a cashmere sleeping bag. And tasted sweeter than refined sugar.

"How crazy is this?" Dylan giggle-shouted over a Destiny's Child song while yanking Kristen through the crowd. Her red hair and emerald green eyes were so vibrant and alive, she almost looked animated.

"Cray-zzzzzy!" Kristen beamed, wondering if she looked animated too. But maybe she just felt that way. Because a world usually reserved for celebrities and the popular girls at OCD was starting to open up to her. All she had to do now was find a way to keep it open. And trading clothes with Merri-Lee Marvil's daughter was the perfect place to start.

The swerving motion of the wheelchair was slightly nauseating. Or was the shame that came from being *pushed* by Mrs. Fossier through a crowd making Alicia's stomach churn? Maybe it was her throbbing ankle? Bloody knee? Destroyed reputation? Stolen Marc Jacobs bag? Or the fact that Skye Hamilton had clogged her voice mail with a barrage of *I have never met anyone more pathetic than you in all my life* messages?

"Hurry!" Alicia whined. The world had seen her wipe out. Did they need to see her puke, too?

"We're almost in our dressing room," Mrs. Fossier cooed, trying to sound compassionate. But it was obvious from her jerky driving that she was upset Alicia had taken down the troupe too.

Mrs. Fossier hit the brakes in front of room C. Brooke and Andrea had gone home. Once Alicia was inside, she could break down in peace. Hot tears stung her brown eyes as the dance teacher jiggled the doorknob. It was locked. She tried it again, this time with more force. Her body odor, a mix of baby powder and canned peaches, was doing nothing for Alicia's delicate condition.

"Coming!" called a phlegm-filled male voice from inside. A second later, the door clicked open. "Can I help you?" He coughed.

An elderly man wearing a tall chef's hat and a white apron that said HERSHEL'S BAKERY across the chest smiled pleasantly.

"I think you're in our dressing room," Mrs. Fossier said slowly and clearly, in case the mix-up was dementia-related.

He glanced at the big letter *C* on the outside of the door. "Nope, this is the one."

Mrs. Fossier folded her arms across her flat chest. "And you are?"

"Hershel Blum." He smiled proudly. "This year's record holder for Biggest Peach Scone. Came in at sixty-one pounds."

"Are you *on* the show?" Mrs. Fossier snapped. "Or catering it?"

"On it." He put his hands on his hips like a satisfied superhero. "Right after the Orlando girl gets her kiss." He shook his head. "She seems a little young to be kissing though, don'tcha think?"

Entertainers hurried by, amped on the adrenaline rush that comes after a live performance. Alicia lowered her gaze, unable to relate. Dogs had replaced her act, and her dressing room had been given to a giant-pastry maker. This captain's ship had sailed. "Let's just go." She sniffed.

"Good idea." Mrs. Fossier kicked the brake release and hurried away from the dressing room like a ticked-off driver who'd just lost a parking spot.

She pulled up beside the performers' food table next to a plate of assorted cheese and a vine of picked-over red grapes. Popping a cheddar cube into her mouth, Mrs. Fossier began to chew-talk.

"I remember a girl . . ." She leaned against the corner of the table, her tongue sweeping the orange cheese bits off her front teeth. "A real dance talent. A starrrrrr." She reached for another cube. "One night, during an opening night performance of *Swan Lake*, she insisted on wearing her new toe shoes. They hadn't been properly worked in and—"

Alicia looked away. The only thing more depressing than wiping out on TV during a once-in-a-lifetime dance performance was listening to a cheese-gobbling grown-up try to make her feel okay about it.

Two cute boys Alicia's age hurried by tugging a pack of dogs toward the backstage exit. Forgetting for a second that she was tear-soaked, swollen, and confined to a wheelchair, Alicia flirt-smiled at them.

"I think she's *falling* for you," said the shaggy blond.

His handsome friend cracked up and the blond wiggled his butt with glee.

Alicia felt that sick feeling come back with the force of a fire hydrant.

Mrs. Fossier was still yapping about some dancer who found real joy in teaching, not performing. She was still chewing. And still smelling like powder and peaches.

Was this really happening?

The world began to swirl. Passing people blurred. Alicia began shaking. Her ears rang and her mouth filled with saliva. A deep-throated burp burst out of her mouth and next thing she knew, her insides turned inside out. All over Mrs. Fossier's Danskin.

"Ahhhhhhh!" The teacher jumped back, slamming into the food table.

"I'm so sorry," Alicia sobbed, tasting bitterness. Her worst nightmare had been realized. She was more pathetic than a washed-up dancer. She was a washed-up dancer in a wheelchair with puke chunks in her lip gloss.

"I'm absolutely covered." Mrs. Fossier splayed her arms and legs like a starfish and waddled to the bathroom like someone who'd just peed her pants.

"There you are!" Len Rivera hurried toward his daughter, his warm brown eyes gleaming with pride.

"Dad, what took you so long?" Alicia sobbed, cleaning herself off with a black-and-gold Merri-Lee napkin. A mix of relief and shame overcame her. "Where's Mom?"

Len leaned down and put an arm around his daughter. He pulled her into his Hugo Boss suit. "They would only let one of us back here." He loosened his navy-and-lavender-striped tie. "And even *that* took a lot of convincing." He rubbed his thumb against his fingertips, implying that the convincing hadn't come cheap. "Are you okay?"

"No." Alicia sobbed harder. "I feel like such a loser."

He lifted her gently out of the chair and pulled her close. She buried her face in her father's lapel and inhaled his spicy scent. As always, he put his hand on her back and tapped like he was burping a baby. In Alicia's head, the rhythmic beats always seemed to say, *You're gonna be fine . . . you're gonna be fine . . . you're gonna be fine . . . you're gonna be fine. . . .*

She lifted her head and breathed deeply. The fresh air helped her throbbing head.

Just then, a man wearing a Merri-Lee Marvil Staff hoodie breezed by and grabbed the wheelchair.

"What are you doing?" Alicia called, hating the desperate sound of her voice.

"I need wheels to move that giant scone to the set," he explained with the urgency of an EMT. "It weighs a ton!"

Alicia opened her mouth to protest but Len pressed a finger against her lips. "Let it go." He took a photo of the man with his free hand. "This will only help our case." He winked a dark brown eye.

"What *case*?" Alicia asked, scooting onto the edge of the table.

Len dangled a Ziploc baggie under his daughter's pouting lip. Inside was a tiny gold shoe, no bigger than a fingernail.

"Thanks." Alicia tried to seem pleased with the cute(ish) get-well gift. But it was pointless. This *pain* would haunt her long after her ankle healed. And no amount of gold would stop it.

"It's *evidence*, my darling." Len gave her the bag. "This is what you slipped on. I intend to send it out for DNA testing, find out who the owner is, and sue them for dance sabotage."

Alicia threw her arms around her father's neck. "Thanks, Daddy." She beamed, finally feeling rescued. "After we win the lawsuit, the papers and news channels will do a story on the scandal. My name will be cleared!" She leaned forward and hugged her father again. Was there anything he couldn't fix?

"Wait . . ." She released him. "Why would anyone want to sabotage *me*?"

"'Scuse me," called a brunette, sauntering toward

them like an actress playing a supermodel. Her black-and-silver dress was Agnès B.'s latest and the perfect choice for a New Year's party. But what promoted her outfit from a "fashion do" to a "fashion debut" were her black (cashmere?) kneesocks with the gold initial pins fastened to the side. Were they doing that in Japan? Whoever this M. B. was, she had the kind of style that made regular girls try harder.

"Are you the one who fell?" M. B. asked, stopping at the table. The stranger's amber eyes held Alicia's with what felt like horizontal gravity.

Alicia lowered her gaze. Was this her new identity? "The girl who fell"?

Len held Alicia back with his arm, like a driver making a sudden stop. "Let me do the talking," he advised.

"Are you a witness?"

"Who isn't?" The girl half smiled. "Everyone saw it. It's probably all over the Internet by now."

"Great," Alicia groaned.

"No, I mean did you see who threw *this*?" Len presented the bag of evidence. "On the stage?"

"My *charm*!" The girl reached for it.

Len pulled the bag away.

"Not so fast," he boomed like a TV detective.

"What are you *doing*?" she screeched. "It's mine!"

"Did *you* throw it?" he asked, this time more forcefully.

"Lennnn," Alicia whined. "*Stop*," she mouthed. It was one thing for her dad to cross-examine crooks in a courtroom. But a "fashion debut" in Agnès B. and cashmere kneesocks? *That* was criminal. Embarrassed, Alicia turned to her swelling ankle. Maybe if she iced long enough her brain would go numb and she could strike this horrifying day from the record.

"Answer, please!" Len insisted, his hands clasped behind his back as he paced in front of a sweating cheese and cracker spread.

"Um, sir," M. B. managed, with a wicked half-smile. "Do you play for Metallica?"

Len knit his thick black brows in confusion. "No."

M. B. paused while three blue bald men hurried by.

"So you're not in Metallica?" she repeated.

Where was she going with this?

"No." Len popped a red grape in his mouth and chewed.

M. B. put her hands on her narrow hips, then cocked her head slightly right. "Then why are you meddling?"

Alicia burst out laughing. Then M. B. did too, obviously pleased (or was it shocked?) by Alicia's reaction.

"There she is!" said a familiar-looking redhead in a pair of Juicys. It was Dylan Marvil and the blond soccer-jock from school. Together? They were all in the fourth grade at Octavian Country Day but never hung out. Dylan was part of the snobby kids-of-celebs clique, which never gave the time of day to dancers with regular parents. And the blond jock was, well . . . a jock.

"You again!" M. B. scanned Dylan's sweats. "Thank Gawd." She sighed, tapping her chest with relief. "Those are much more flattering."

Dylan smiled. Her hair was half-straight and half-curly. A trend, Alicia prayed, that would die before the New Year. "Thanks."

"For what?" asked M. B.

"You're the only one who told me the truth about those pants," Dylan explained, then smiled at Alicia. "You're lucky to have a friend like her."

"Oh, she's not my friend," Alicia corrected. "We just met."

"Hey." The blonde waved. *Did she realize her leather pants were ripped?* "I'm Kristen. I just wanted to give this back to—"

"Massie." She smiled. "Massie Block."

"I have one too." Dylan placed a tiny gold pig in Massie's palm.

"Ehmagawd, yay!" Massie slid the charms onto the chain, then smiled at the girls. "I've been looking for these all night!"

Alicia, longing to be part of their circle, yanked the

Ziploc out of her father's hand and handed it to Massie. "Here ya go."

"Thank you!" Massie opened her arms, welcoming Alicia into the fold. It smelled like Chanel No. 19.

Energy passed through them, like electric thread stringing needles, binding them together and pulling them close.

Did they feel it too?

"Two minutes until midnight!" called a stage manager.

"Happy New Year!" Dylan burped.

The girls burst out laughing.

"Hey, wanna go watch the clutch drop?" Massie tucked her bracelet in the pocket of her dress.

"Yeah!" Kristen clapped.

"We can hang with my mom," Dylan offered. "She'll be at the very top. It's the best view."

Alicia looked at her father, silently asking if she could go. He wink-nodded yes.

The girls helped Alicia off the table and encouraged her to lean on them for support.

With their help, she limp-hopped into the party, no longer feeling like the girl who fell. But rather, the one who got back up again.

Thanks to Dylan—who told her sisters they looked bloated and should stay away from the cameras—space opened up on the hydraulic platform. It was tight, but Merri-Lee, her two-man crew, and the four girls were all smiles as they rose above the awestruck crowd and through the hole in the roof. They stopped beside the gold-and-black-beaded YSL clutch, surrounded by stars and the navy night sky.

Frigid wind blew their hair wild, yet no one seemed to mind.

"Where are your coats?" Merri-Lee asked, pinch-closing the top of her white fur bomber jacket.

The girls exchanged a *why would we ever, in a billion years, wear coats on TV?* look, and Massie knew she had found her soul mates. Unlike the Ahnnabees, who entered a black-tie party dressed like bubble-wrapped Easter eggs, these girls had style.

"Whaddaya mean, the Orlando girl is *gone*?" Merri-Lee turned away, pressing a finger against her earpiece. "She's supposed to kiss ThRob in less than a minute!"

She looked at her crew and rolled her green eyes. "Her parents *took* her? . . . Did you get it on camera? . . . Great! . . . Then roll *that* at midnight!"

Massie giggled at the thought of some poor girl's parents dragging her away from the biggest opportunity of her life. "What an LBR," she muttered.

"What's an LBR?" asked Alicia.

"Loser beyond repair," Massie stated.

The girls cracked up. Massie half smiled, unsure whether they were laughing at her or with her.

"Can I use that?" Alicia's big brown eyes widened with hope.

"Me too?" Dylan asked.

"And me?" Kristen wondered.

"Sure." Massie beamed. Ahnna always thought that term was stupid.

Not that Ahnna mattered anymore. A new year was about to start. And with a new year came new ideas. Ideas from her notebook that Massie resolved to turn into realities. Things like:

* Weekly sleepovers at my house.

* Lists about what was in and what was out.

* Rating systems. Possibly out of ten. To gauge looks and outfit-fabulousness.

* Award points for gossip.

* Carpools to school, chauffeured by Isaac.

* Carpools to the mall, chauffeured by Isaac.

* Carpools to parties, chauffeured by Isaac.

* Carpools to spray-tan appointments, chauffeured by Isaac.

* Carpools to Starbucks, chauffeured by Isaac.

* What Would You Rather challenges.

* Boy/girl parties.

* Wardrobe summits.

* Hair summits.

* Makeup summits.

* Accessory summits.

* Product summits.

* School supply summits.

* Technology summits.

* Shopping summits.

* Social invitation acceptance summits.

* Favorite color summits.

* Favorite snack summits.

* Favorite celeb summits.

* Crush summits.

* Party summits.

* Hair removal summits.

* Hair extension summits.

* Mani-pedi summits.

* Eyewear summits.

* A black pug named Bean.

* Designated lunch table, with me at the head.

* Walking order, with me in the middle.

* Headquarters for GLUs (Girls Like Us).

* Bedroom makeover. Royal purple, please.

* Loser makeovers.

* Spa days.

* Vacation packing lists.

* Slang that only they would understand, like LBR, GLU, beta, HART, jobby, POTI, POTO, sand-me-down . . .

* And of course, NO MORE THAN FOUR.

"Fifteen seconds until midnight!" Merri-Lee announced.

The camera operator lifted a giant Sony onto his shoulder and flicked the switch. A red light illuminated on the side of the lens. "We're live."

Below, the crowd was getting anxious, like caged animals sensing a storm.

Noisemakers were buzzing. Streamers were being tossed. Champagne corks were popping.

Outside the hangar, the less fortunate were already hugging, probably for warmth. Ribbons of air billowed from their frostbitten noses as they lifted their heads in reverence to the giant designer clutch.

"Here we go!" Merri-Lee shouted into her mic, her voice amplified throughout the party. "Ten! . . . Nine! . . ."

Everyone shout-counted along while the hydraulic platform lowered in perfect time with the sparkling Yves clutch. Massie waved at the crowd below, like a queen overlooking her royal subjects.

Ehmagawd! This was the moment Hermia was talking about. Massie's palms tingled with joy. She was finally feeling *it*! Flanked by fashionable girls and waving at the masses while they literally looked up to her. This was her fate! She was living her destiny. She was . . .

The platform lowered a few more inches.

. . . *WAIT!* Would her reign expire once they reached the ground? Was this what she had been working toward her entire life? A ten-second ride beside a giant hand-bag? Was this it for her *it*?

Massie reached into the pocket of her dress and gripped her purple stone, silently asking it if there was any more to this seemingly magical night.

"Eight! . . . Seven! . . . Six! . . ." Dylan count-shouted at the crowd below.

Alicia wiped hair out of her lip gloss.

"Five! . . . Four! . . ."

Kristen covered her exposed butt with her free hand.

"Three! . . . Two! . . ."

The bag and the platform touched down in the center of the dance floor.

"One! . . . HAPPY NEW YEAR!"

A live performance from ThRob rocked the house via satellite while everyone embraced.

The girls crammed together again for another four-way hug. They melded together like different-colored metals.

"Stawp!" demanded a familiar girl's voice. "Stawp right now!"

Massie broke away from the group and turned around. Shauna, Briana, and Lana stood behind their plaid leader. Their arms folded across their chests, eyes squinted in contempt. They seemed still compared to the celebratory chaos swirling around them.

"The *Ahnnabees*?" Kristen whispered.

"Kr-isten," Ahnna hissed.

Massie gasped. "You *know* them?"

"Unfortunately." Kristen rolled her eyes.

Alicia giggled. "It's the Mad Plaider."

"If they stood in a line, they'd be a caterplaider," Kristen joked.

"Burrrrrr-berrrry!" Dylan burped.

"Burberry dresses, no punch-backs." Massie playfully punched her new friends.

They all cracked up and exchanged high fives.

"Um, yeah, that's so funny I forgot to *ditch you*!" Black eyeliner was smudged under Ahnna's eyes and her forehead glistened with sweat. She looked like she had just been microwaved. "I wanted to leave you here, but my dad wouldn't let me."

Massie stared at her blankly. Hadn't they already left her?

"We're driving you home tonight, re-mem-ber?"

"Oh," Massie mumbled, her spirits falling like the YSL bag. She felt like Cinderella, forced to return to her humdrum life after a night at the ball.

"*My* dad can take you home," Alicia offered.

"He can?" Massie's insides jumped up and high-fived each other.

"Given." Alicia smiled, looking more beautiful than Ahnna ever could.

"And what are you gonna do at school?" Ahnna asked. "You know, when you have no friends."

Shauna, Lana, and Brianna giggled.

"She's transferring to OCD," Dylan chimed in. "So she can be with us."

"We don't have to wear those ugly plaid uniforms you're trying to pass off as designer, either," Alicia added. "We can wear whatever we want."

"Personal style is encouraged," Dylan told Massie.

Alicia giggle-nodded in agreement.

Ahnna rolled her eyes while roving cameras captured the hugs and kisses being given out all around the party.

Really? Massie's mind expanded like an elastic waistband. There would be no end to the clothing combinations she could try. Outfits! Accessories! Boots! Monday, Tuesday, Wednesday, Thursday, Friday, Saturday, Sunday! Her life as a weekend wardrobe warrior would be over. She'd finally be able to showcase her flair seven days a week. Bust out of that itchy restrictive PMS uniform like the Incredible Hulk. Let her fashion flag fly!

"And school doesn't start for another three weeks, so you have tons of time to shop," Alicia added.

Massie dug a silver-polished fingernail into her palm. Was this really happening?

"Me and V can go with you if you want?" Dylan made two *V*'s with her fingers.

"Who's V?" Massie asked, hoping it wasn't Dylan's BFF. These girls were too good to share.

"Visa." Dylan shrugged matter-of-factly, her emerald green eyes shimmering like sun on the Caribbean Sea.

"I'll bring . . ." Alicia struggled to make an *A* and an *X* with her fingers. She looked like a break-dancer trying to master sign language. "AmEx."

"I can help you with the school application," Kristen offered.

"Really?" Massie asked, searching their eyes for glimpses of insincerity and finding none. Instead, she saw three girls smile-nodding. They seemed as genuinely grateful to have met her as she was to have met them. "I'm in!" she shouted over the sounds of blowers, kisses, and laughter.

"Yayyyy!" The girls hugged again.

Lana, Briana, Shauna, and Ahnna's jaws hung slack, like they were watching a movie about skinned kittens. A movie that needed to end.

"Um, Ahnna, are you a piñata?" Massie asked.

"No," Ahnna scoffed.

"Then, um, why are you hanging around?"

Alicia, Dylan, and Kristen burst out laughing.

"That's it!" gasped Ahnna. "Your PMS days are

over!" The Ahnnabees stormed off in a plaid fury. Angry and out of sync with the celebration, they fought their way toward the exit, vanishing like a toxic fart in a lily-scented summer breeze.

"Thank Gawd." Massie beamed, turning her back on them, this time for good.

"You know," she mused, linking arms with her new friends, "we should have a sleepover every Friday night at my house, to honor the night we first met."

"Done," Alicia said.

"Done," Dylan said.

"And done," Kristen said.

For the first time in her life, Massie felt complete. No more trying to sell good ideas to bad people. From now on she would be heard, respected, revered. She had attracted the necessary pieces and was finally feeling *it*! She would start fresh at a new school and transform her girls into the stuff legendary cliques are made of. Hermia had been right about everything. . . .

Almost.

Only four pieces had come together, not five. But Massie decided to let that go. She had bigger things to worry about. Like what to name their group. But she'd worry about that tomorrow. Tonight all she wanted to think about was the endless amounts of fun that lay ahead. No fights. No stress. No pressure. No joiners!

Arms still linked, Massie led her new friends into the heart of the party. Like a human charm bracelet they all moved as one, each girl linked to the next. Each girl a valuable piece of gold.

After seven minutes of fussing with the timer on the digital camera, the flash went off.

"Cheese." Claire tried to smile. But it was too late. Her commemorative New Year's Eve photo had been taken. Instead of being surrounded by her best friends, donning homemade crowns and sugar-induced grins, she was alone on her bed. Glitter was sprinkled everywhere. Her Hello Kitty boom box was totaled. Discarded costumes lay in heaps like land mines. Sugar snacks hardened like unwanted candy on a movie theater floor. And scraps of paper, scissors, and different-colored glue sticks were strewn across her white shag rug. This was how Claire had left her room when they snuck out. Back when she had hope. Back when she was happy. Back when she was a *winner*.

The sound of the local news playing and replaying the clip of her being dragged away by her parents seeped through her lime green bedroom walls.

"Oh, that poor girl," snickered Carmen Ballucci, Kissimmee's famed anchorwoman-slash-1992-pageant-winner. "Let's watch that again, shall we?"

"You are so bad," chided her coanchor, Benton New-market.

"I can't help it." She giggled. "It's so—"

"Hilarious?" offered Benton.

"Yes." She beamed. "Roll the clip! Last time, I promise."

"Ugh!" Claire smacked her daisy-covered duvet in frustration. She could practically see Carmen's goofy smile. Her fake white teeth horsing forward. Her heavily shadowed lids fluttering with delight. Her flipped blond bangs bouncing with glee.

Claire covered her head with a pillow, but it didn't matter. She could still hear everything. The humiliating scene marked her brain like a giant skull-and-crossbones tattoo.

"What's happening?" asked Theo.

"Wait." Rob said. *"Is this a payback prank?"*

"I wish," Claire mumbled.

"Looks like you're gonna have to kiss something else at midnight," Judi Lyons snapped. *"Perverts,"* she shouted.

"Mom!" Claire gasped. *"Don't do this to me!"*

"I'd hate to be *her* father," Benton the newscaster stated.

Claire's dad pounded the wall. "Tell me about it!" he shouted.

"I'm sorry, okay!" Claire pounded back as if the walls

were an extension of her own stupid self. The self that convinced her she could get away with such an elaborate stunt. The self that wished, more than anything, that she had.

Her mother pounded back twice. "You'll be sorry all right, when we send you to *boarding school.*"

Claire rolled her eyes. Did they not think the major embarrassment that came with having the incident played and replayed on the local news was punishment enough?

"Think they mean it?" tweeted a little voice. It was coming from under her bed.

Claire leaned over the side, white-blond hair falling around her face like a collapsed parachute. She locked eyes with a small redhead in Batman pajamas. He was lying on his back, mechanic style.

"Todd!" Claire whisper-shouted. "What're you doing in here?"

Her brother crawled out and joined his sister on the bed. Claire lifted herself up to face him, her anger melting like a ChapStick in the glove compartment. Even though she was beyond tired of his eavesdropping, it was nice to have some company.

"Do you really think they'll send you to boarding school?" he asked, like he'd actually miss her.

"No way." She smiled strongly for both of them.

"Those places are full of rich snobs." Claire bit her thumbnail. "They're just trying to scare me." She nodded with certainty. "They'll forget all about this by Valentine's Day."

Todd sighed. Claire could smell his minty toothpaste. "Think they'll change their mind about not letting me watch SpongeBob for a month?"

Claire shook her head no. "Sorry. I know this is all my fault."

"I'll forgive you if I can have . . ." Todd scanned the bedroom with renewed hope. His hazel eyes landed on the silver bowl of gummies. *"Those."* He pointed at the oily lump.

"Fine." Claire giggled without smiling.

Todd jumped off the bed and claimed his prize. He slurped down the worms like spaghetti while Claire tended to her trashed room.

Sadly, she began scooping up the debris. The sooner she cleaned, the sooner she could put this whole mess behind her. She leaned forward to pick up her trash can and . . . *thud.* The red jewelry box that ThRob had given her fell out of her dress pocket.

"What is that?" Todd chew-asked.

"Nothing," she lied, turning away from her brother, suddenly wishing she were alone. Alone to cherish what was left of Theo and Rob.

She sat down on the end of her bed, surrounded by red organza, the way Scarlett might have after Rhett left her, and slowly opened her consolation prize. Inside, resting in cotton, lay a tiny silver microphone charm. It blurred and melted behind her tears, as she thought about what could have been had she not been caught. Unable to withstand the torture of what-ifs, Claire snapped the box shut and hid it away in her desk drawer, desperate to leave this terrible night in the past.

Who knew? Maybe some day she'd regift it.

```
┌ ─────────────────────────────────────────── ┐
│                                              │
│                                              │
│                                              │
│              ACKNOWLEDGMENTS                 │
│                                              │
│                                              │
│                                              │
│                                              │
└ ─────────────────────────────────────────── ┘
```

Since this is the Clique prequel and I went back in time, I would like to acknowledge the people who helped grow this series from the very beginning. In order of when we met.*

1. The voices in my head**
2. Ben Shrank
3. Richard Abate
4. Josh Bank
5. Les Morgenstein
6. Lynn Weingarten
7. Cindy Eagan
8. Sara Shandler
9. Lanie Davis
10. Alex Kohner

*If this was in order of importance and brilliance all of your names would be number one and no one would be able to read them.

**Okay, fine, so I didn't actually meet the "voices in my head," but this is my acknowledgment and I can make whatever claims I want. Even if they don't make sense.

If at first you don't succeed, you're not an Alpha.

ALPHAS

Don't miss the second ah-mazing novel in Lisi Harrison's ALPHAS series, MOVERS AND FAKERS, coming April 2010.

Welcome to Poppy.

A poppy is a beautiful blooming red flower
(like the one on the spine of this book). It is also
the name of the home of your favorite books.

Poppy takes the real world and makes it
a little funnier, a little more fabulous.

Poppy novels are wild, witty, and inspiring.
They were written just for you.

So sit back, get comfy, and pick a Poppy.

poppy

www.pickapoppy.com